Also by Steven Key Meyers

Novels

My Hollywood Memoir and Other Fiction
(includes *Sidestep*, *Big Luck* and *Save the Max Man!*)

That's My Story
(includes *The Last Posse*)

Family Romance

My Mad Russian: Three Tales
(includes *Another's Fool* and *I Remember Caramoor*)

The Wedding on Big Bone Hill
(includes *Junkie, Indiana*)

Springtime in Siena
(includes *The Man Who Owned New York*)

All That Money

Good People

Plays & Screenplays

*A Journal of the Plague Year,
and Other Plays and Adaptations*

The Midhurst Lashes
Adapted from the novels of A.C. Swinburne

Nonfiction

*The Man in the Balloon:
Harvey Joiner's Wondrous 1877*

The Holy Hugs

of Father S.

a novel

Steven Key Meyers

The Holy Hugs of Father S.

Copyright © 2024 Steven Key Meyers
All rights reserved

ISBN 979-8-9850215-6-1

No part of this publication may be reproduced, stored in a retrieval system or transmitted in any form or by any means, electronic, mechanical, recording or otherwise, without the prior written permission of the author.

Except for historical characters treated fictionally, all characters appearing in this work are fictitious. Any resemblance to real persons, living or dead, is coincidental.

**SMASH
&GRAB**
PRESS

The Holy Hugs
of Father S.

For my two friends, in petto

We are amazed to find how often a man who would be behind bars if he were not a priest is entrusted with the *cura animarum*.

— Father Gerald M.C. Fitzgerald (1894-1969), writing to the Bishop of Manchester, N.H. in 1957

—THE HOLY HUGS OF FATHER S.—

1.

MONSIGNOR BRANNICK ALWAYS bought his cars from the Pontiac dealer in his old parish in Northwest Washington, trading them in every two years. He assured his auxiliary, Father Schmidt, that if he wanted a new car (and—he sniffed—St. Jude's parishioners would probably appreciate his replacing that battered old Ford of his), they'd give him a good deal, too. Perhaps on a nice Bonneville?

But Father Schmidt didn't want a nice Bonneville. He had his eye on an altogether cooler vehicle. He conceded that Monsignor's Grand Prix in midnight blue suited *him* exactly—fenders swelling above wheel skirts, the sheet-metal equivalent to his swirling monsignorial cassock with purple buttons—but said he preferred to buy within the parish.

In fact, he was talking with a bass in his choir, Mr. Grimes, sales manager at the Chrysler-Plymouth-Dodge dealership on Georgia Avenue in Wheaton, who showed him a brand-new 1966 Plymouth Fury III coupe that seized his heart.

At first sight several evenings earlier he expressed horror at the paint job.

"But it's *purple,* Mr. Grimes!"

"That's the lights, Father. No, it's blue, almost baby blue. Best color for this model, I swear. Can put you in it on very easy terms."

"I'll pay cash when the time comes, Mr. Grimes."

"All the better, Father."

Father Schmidt returned by daylight to confirm the Plymouth's handsome blue (carried through to the carpeting, padded dashboard and vinyl upholstery grained to look and feel like leather), added three miles to the odometer's eight, and agreed to buy it.

Today was the day. After lunch Father picked up his checkbook and drove the Ford out.

At the dealership, Mr. Grimes strode outdoors and took Father to where stood the gleaming Fury, headlights stacked, the upper ones jutting ahead. The car's stance had it doing 60 standing still.

"Here it is, Father, washed and waxed. You like?"

"It's beautiful, Mr. Grimes."

They walked around it, Mr. Grimes caressing it and murmuring about its features. Then they stepped indoors to sign the papers. Mr. Grimes awarding the Ford a big fat trade-in allowance, Father Schmidt wrote a check for the balance, acquiring his $3,300 car with radio, white-wall tires, power brakes, power steering, air conditioning and undercoating for a tad under $2,500 (it cleaned him out). Mr. Grimes said he didn't make many such deals, but credited the Man Upstairs with suggesting this one, and professed himself satisfied.

"Enjoy it, Father. It's a fine car, and you look good in it."

—THE HOLY HUGS OF FATHER S.—

Father shook his hand, got behind the wheel and, pausing only to tune the radio to WINX and pull out a push button to preset the station, waved as he turned onto Georgia Avenue.

He couldn't resist just driving. Out in the countryside, only a few miles away, he began taking twisting roads at random through the March landscape. Spring was advancing, the trees flaunting new leaves. The white fences of horse country flew past as he shot forward: 230 horsepower, twice the Ford's. Mr. Grimes said to take it easy during the break-in period, but that when he accelerated to do it confidently. The radio played the Four Seasons' *Working My Way Back to You*. Father's expertise lay in liturgical music, but for driving he liked rock'n'roll or R&B.

Excited, Father also felt nostalgic. He'd been fond of the Ford he abandoned at the dealership. He bought it shortly after arriving at St. Abigail's, the girls' school in Northwest, a 1954 model only two years old, and took to it, too, though it was never the flashiest car, nor the fastest; no, not a fast car.

A year before that, at his first assignment as a newly-ordained priest—St. Christopher's High School, also in Northwest—he was still driving his own father's 1940 Chevy, a car he despised and one that won no admiration from his students.

A long time ago now, though ten years—eleven?—didn't mean that what happened at St. Chris hadn't happened. No, it happened all right, unfortunately.

He still thought about it when he masturbated. Which wasn't often, for masturbation is a sin and Father faithfully confessed his sins to Monsignor, and that was an embarrassing one to have to mention. But his body—the body God Himself gave him!—sometimes compelled him to do it, to think back and find gratification in what he undeniably did—though surely with no harm done?—in St. Chris' gymnasium late one afternoon when, a young priest teaching music, math and some gym classes, he lingered with his favorite student after everybody else went home.

Ray, a lively lad with a blond flattop, was 15 years old.

Ray started it.

"Want to wrestle, Father? Unless you think you can't handle it?"

Back and forth for a bit—Ray was a cheeky kid, fun to talk to, his insouciance irresistible—until Father, compelled by desire to say out loud what he really wanted, remarked, "I'll wrestle you, Ray—but only Greco-Roman style."

"How's that, Father?"

His mouth suddenly dry, eyes looking aside, Father couldn't say.

"You mean *nude*, Father?" asked Ray. "*Naked*, Father? Won't help, you're going *down*."

The boy was that spunky. He and Father shucked shirts, pants, everything. When he summoned the memory, Father saw in slow, *slow* motion the revelations leading to Ray's perfected nudity, standing there grinning, legs reaching to the power of his hips, the fact of his cock, the vulnerability of his belly, the story of his chest.

Usually in recalling it Father ejaculated before he could replay their tussling together, that long process of trying— but not *too* hard—to pin Ray, their trading of positions, muttering, groaning, their mutual enjoyment (Father was

—THE HOLY HUGS OF FATHER S.—

sure of it!) before the need to *take* Ray, *penetrate* him, overmastered him, and he got rough until, before he could quite accomplish it, the boy—scared now—slithered out of his grasp, scooped up his clothes and ran off.

Father Schmidt knew he'd gone too far—in fact, sinned. *Probably* sinned, though surely more a sin of *intention* than *deed*? (Had he confessed it? Doubtless he had.)

Never saw Ray again; overnight the boy switched, nobody knew why, to Bethesda–Chevy Chase High School. But something must have got back to someone (such was his dark suspicion), because Father soon found himself at St. Abigail's, loosed among the young ladies to teach math and direct their choir. Its choir was never so celebrated as under Father Schmidt, performing at the dedication of the National Shrine of the Immaculate Conception and frequently traveling to Baltimore and Richmond. God knows, for three long years he did his best, before having the unexpected good fortune to be selected by Archbishop Patrick O'Boyle's great favorite, Monsignor Brannick, as auxiliary priest and choirmaster for his new parish.

St. Jude's was carved out from two existing parishes in the fastest-growing part of the fast-growing Maryland suburbs. The Archbishop in naming Monsignor its pastor gave him the mission of building a showcase church and school. Monsignor, knowing how prestigious a fine boys choir is, vowed to have the best in the region, so engaged Father Schmidt, who would also do the parish scutwork. In addition, he recruited sisters from a progressive Minnesota order of Franciscan nuns to teach in the school.

Turning around, Father eventually hit the Beltway, got on and worked up to speeds the Ford never knew. No more losing face in traffic! Beneath his glasses he kept his expression sedate and priestly, but inside felt let loose and free.

Nobody ever called Father Schmidt handsome. Of middle size, 39 years old—"same age as Jack Benny," he'd taken to joking—he had acne-scarred cheeks and weak eyes. Hence the severe black-framed glasses that were his feature. When caught out without them, his face tended to look embarrassed. The glasses precluded much expressiveness anyway, but behind them his face was usually almost as rigid, a mask showing not much at all.

Except at choir practice, except with his boys. Music represented the best of Father Schmidt. He was perfectly sincere about making music to glorify the Lord. What he was able to do with his choir *(sometimes)*—after the hard labor of recruiting and instructing and rehearsing—was to construct intricate but powerful structures of song that demonstrated—*illuminated*—the beauty of God's creation; build a crystalline portal of sound out of boys' and men's voices, a portal that for a time (the length of a hymn, anyway) opened to the glorious world awaiting us and reconciled all hearers (he hoped!) to God and Mother Church.

Exiting at University Boulevard, he crawled along Teagers Mill Road, which, despite its widening, seemed slower every day, so fast was local growth. A few blocks from St. Jude's he passed its rectory, in Teagers Mill Estates; a new rectory was finally nearing completion behind St. Jude's playground.

School was letting out when Father Schmidt returned, a few minutes later than he'd intended, children coming out to meet their carpools or board the waiting buses that would continue to the nearby public school. Some walked

—THE HOLY HUGS OF FATHER S.—

or bicycled home, a few even roller-skated.

Father's new Fury caused a stir as he parked in the circle. He accepted compliments and promised future rides, but it was time for choir practice, so he strolled indoors to the choir room as choristers streamed in: Sixteen boys, five from 8th grade, five from 7th, six from 5th, including his prize soprano, Johnny Capistrano, possessor of the purest voice Father ever heard. None of the men, including Mr. Grimes, could make it to weekday practice; they caught up on Saturday. The room, cinder-block walls a glossy yellow, was a classroom like the others, but with folding chairs instead of desks.

Father took up his stance facing the boys in their school uniforms of gray corduroy pants—mostly too short and too tight—long-sleeved white shirts and plaid ties.

"Page 117," he said, and they turned to it in their hymnals. Seeing in his mind's eye Gregorian chant's square notation, Father lifted his arms and the room filled with an ancient Easter sequence, feelingly sung by ordinary American boys molded into a choir he'd put up against any:

> *Victimae paschali laudes*
> *immolent Christiani...*

They were in good voice today, the 8th graders especially. Father heard more power from them at every practice—the intoxicating sound of hormones. They were getting so grown up and good-looking, too, the baby fat of their cheeks thinning, faces modeling newly adult expressions as they sang.

Today the tallest boy, Jeff Osborne, caught his eye, his

expression dreamy, body tilted forward to inject meaning into the text. He was going to be very good-looking someday. Here in the practice room any temptation Father Schmidt felt he offered up like a good Catholic—turned it to God's own purpose, shaping and projecting His songs of praise.

After some final pitch exercises, he ended the day's session.

"Good practice, boys!"

Shepherding them out, his work day over, Father was itchy to keep driving, so took the Fury back up Teagers Mill to the rectory driveway and, leaving the engine running but turning the radio off, ran inside to ask Monsignor if he'd like a ride in his new car before dinner.

Monsignor surprised him by saying, "Sure," clapping his skullcap to his head and getting in.

Father backed carefully into Teagers Mill Road.

"*Nice*," said Monsignor, breathing in the new-car smell. "Certainly a step up from the Ford."

"Engine's a Mopar 318 V-8," announced Father, playfully pasting them to the backs of their seats. They passed St. Jude's and its neighboring horse farm and, across the road, two brick mansions surviving from before the Civil War atop knolls at the center of horse meadows. Soon they were in the countryside. Always aware that they might be seen, recognized, called to account, they comported themselves accordingly, sitting together expressionlessly.

Father hoped they were effective colleagues, but knew they weren't friends. Though he privately thought his superior resembled his beloved Irish potatoes in every respect—head, nose, belly, buttocks—Monsignor held

— *THE HOLY HUGS OF FATHER S.* —

himself out as somehow superior to his auxiliary, whether by virtue of family or education or, as Father put it to himself, simply by virtue of virtue.

It grated. So it wasn't very nice a few weeks back when Monsignor criticized Father's table manners.

"Father, you eat like a toddler in a high chair!" he thundered at dinner one evening, arms flying and fingers splayed in imitation. "It's enough to make one sick!"

Then he kindly demonstrated how it should be done — not as an open-mouthed grabbing affair, food ending up everywhere, but a neat tabletop operation, deft manipulation of cutlery at the plate allowing discreet transmission of morsels to the mouth.

It hurt Father Schmidt's feelings. Coming from a big family where he had to fight for food, he was sorry, but thought Monsignor could be a little more tolerant.

Often one or the other had dinner invitations out, but not tonight; tonight they would eat their housekeeper's meal, tucked in the oven beneath a moistened towel before Mrs. Logan left for the day. But separately.

As the lovely old countryside rushed past, Monsignor sighed, *"We Are Christ."*

Father finally prompted, "Yes?"

"Lobbied for this movie. Let's hope I don't live to regret it."

"Can't wait," said Father.

"Are you ready? The choir, I mean?"

"Oh yes. Chosen some of our livelier hymns, ones the congregation knows."

"Good," said Monsignor, and sighed again. "It's a great honor, I know it is, but it's going to be exhausting, too. Guess we can announce it any time. Want the church packed for the filming."

"Oh, there'll be no trouble on that score. People will want to be part of it."

"Let's hope."

They passed through a crossroads of shanties that dated back 100 or 150 years, store windows only recently denuded of NO COLORED and NO NEGROES signs.

"The stakes seem higher with this vacancy," Monsignor said. He didn't have to spell out that he meant Auxiliary Bishop Philip Hannon's recent elevation to Archbishop of New Orleans. "O'Boyle needs a new sidekick. Lord knows he's taking his time making up his mind, but everything counts."

It was a heady thought that Monsignor's elevation could only mean good things for Father Schmidt, too—likely as the next pastor of St. Jude's, probably as a Monsignor himself: *The Singing Monsignor.*

They looped home by way of Randolph Road, Monsignor saying, "Well, whatever happens, it's an honor, this film."

"Choir's ready to do its part."

As they pulled up behind the Grand Prix—Father fighting the urge to show off the power brakes by slamming them into the windshield—Monsignor said, "It's a very nice car, Father. No idea you were so sporty."

2.

FATHER BOUGHT HIS Fury on Thursday, March 10, 1966, the day Washington-area parochial high schools mailed their letters of acceptance or regret.

Friday the 11th, then, St. Jude's 8th graders were wild with anticipation. After lunch their playground wars took on new brutality. For six years — since the school opened — the boys had squared off into gangs at recess and charged one another in rough kidnapping raids, dashing past the girls on the swings, the teeter-totter, the jungle gym to fight all comers.

Jeff Osborne never cared to lead a gang, but always was his leader's number two, whoever that year's leader happened to be, and relished working the strings from behind. One front tooth had a chip out from when he was captured and tied up in a broken swing's chains and the end of one struck him in the mouth. It gave him, when he grinned, a mildly piratical look.

After recess Sister Madonna liked to cool down her students by reading to them, but today she allowed anyone who wanted to see if their letters had arrived to call home from the pay phone next to the church doors.

A dozen girls and boys took up her offer, Jeff among them. It felt free and adult to move past classrooms filled with murmurs of instruction—50 kids in every one!—and bump down the hallway, white shirts or plaid skirts and vests billowing. Those of his male classmates who didn't want to go to public high school had applied to Good Shepherd, the local Christian Brothers school, but Jeff had no wish to go there. Instead, at his father's suggestion, he applied to Garrett Preparatory School, the famous Jesuit institution.

Jeff had no great desire to go there, either. For six months past he'd daily probed students' faces in Prep's catalog, and every time failed to see himself as one of them. But Prep was famously selective and the idea of being rejected repelled him.

They took turns dialing to see whether the letter had arrived *(it had!)* and if the envelope was thin or thick. Those from Good Shepherd or St. Catherine, the girls school, were all thick—a credit to St. Jude's first graduating class.

Everyone looking on, listening in, Jeff called home.

"Hello, Mother. . .? Did the letter from Garrett Prep arrive?" Yes, it had. "Is it thin or thick?" She wasn't sure, couldn't say. "Well, please go ahead and open it, then."

Jeff heard paper being torn.

"Oh!" Carol said. "Let's see. . . You were. . . It says. . . Let me read it. . . *Yes*: 'offer you a place in the Class of 1970.' Yes, honey, you were *accepted!*"

Jeff beamed. A bit of drama, but it worked out, made for a gratifying moment after the ordeal of tests, essays and the Headmaster's interview.

—THE HOLY HUGS OF FATHER S.—

"Oh, and honey," Carol added, "Daddy's coming home today. Isn't that wonderful?"

"To die?" thought Jeff, but asked, "Is he better?"

"Of course he is!"

His friends seemed pleased with his acceptance to Prep, and Sister Madonna certainly was.

At choir practice Jeff was distracted—his father coming home?—but so were some of the other boys. Sister Madonna assured them that acceptance at their chosen schools meant a lot to St. Jude's, but Father Schmidt grew impatient, even singled out Jeff as needing to work on a certain passage of chant.

Afterwards he walked home. It was only two miles, and walking let him retire from the world to think about whatever he wished.

And the walk had its picturesque elements. Wheaton was an overlay of the brand-new over the really old. Jeff knew that the landmarks along the way—that horse farm, those upright old mansions—were doomed. In a few years there would be dozens of new houses instead; no longer would horses rush to the fence to exchange greetings.

After the horse farm came Brown's Lane. Menace appeared to lurk among the tumbledown houses of the extended, practically aboriginal family Brown, rumored to be inbred and regarded with alarm by their latecomer suburban neighbors. Sometimes Jeff saw young Browns riding their bikes—one had a motorbike!—sneering like juvenile delinquents.

Almost opposite was the entrance to Storybook Forest, Jeff's family's community. He'd heard it called "where the rich kids live," but its houses mostly were rather modest. What set it apart from Teagers Mill Estates—where Jeff's family used to live, and where every house's quarter-acre was allotted a sapling in front and another in the rear — were the trees preserved from the old forest on lots ranging upwards from an acre. There was cachet to living amongst the trees.

He was thinking about his acceptance to Prep and how it helped with the fact of his father's coming home.

Denton Osborne was a journalist enjoying a successful career. Home from war in the Pacific, he entered J-school, then landed newspaper jobs out West before joining ORBS Magazine as a correspondent in its Chicago bureau. A few years later came the summons to Washington, where, covering Congress and the White House, he rapidly began racking up cover stories.

Then he got sick.

What Jeff knew was sketchy, and he wasn't one for asking questions he dreaded the answers to. It was as though his Dad were off on an out-of-town reporting trip. Covering civil rights he'd spent half of 1957 in Little Rock, and as ORBS's man following Nixon on the 1960 campaign trail, and LBJ in '64, he was gone weeks at a time, then home for as little as twelve hours before heading out again.

But Dent wasn't on a reporting trip. He'd had an operation — supposedly a success — at the Cleveland Clinic, followed by extended convalescent care.

Now he was coming home.

When Jeff's father was home things were different and, if he was writing, difficult. Taking over the dining room table in the brick split level made the whole upstairs a quiet zone. If he occupied his den downstairs, across from Jeff's room, the quiet zone included the family room and its TV. The writing — in longhand on yellow pads — was the center, the focus of the house, even as Dent robotically wandered upstairs and down, seeing nothing as he continued writing in his head.

Jeff's mother would type what needed to be typed on grainy copy paper. Dinner on such days was frozen pot pies or fish sticks or a quick run to the new McDonald's in Glenmont; if they went out to eat with his Dad thus preoccupied, it was just to Wheaton Plaza's faux-Tudor steakhouse with diamond-paned windows and red-shaded lights.

Turning down Trent Lane — a cul-de-sac of seven houses, two occupied by CIA men — Jeff saw an ambulance in his driveway. No one was in it, but two sturdy men came out the front door, followed by Carol thanking them.

His heart fell, and then he felt guilty about it.

The ambulance drove away.

"You can go in and see Daddy," Carol said as he brushed past and headed downstairs.

"In a minute."

He used the bathroom and changed his clothes, pulling on jeans and a T-shirt, stuffing his uniform pants and shirt in the hamper and reminding himself to iron a week's worth by Sunday night.

Then he was ready. Going upstairs, he found his parents' bedroom door open. Between the bed and windows his father lay in a hospital bed, the back cranked up to help him see outdoors. Past the lawn stood woods, light from the western sky leaking through the leaves.

"Hi, Daddy."

His Dad turned his face. "Hey, Sport, how goes it?"

Jeff went over, shook his hand and sat down on the other bed. He hadn't seen his father since before the operation. Though not expressly forbidden to visit, neither parent had encouraged it, and Dent meanwhile refused visits from friends and colleagues.

"Why?" Jeff had asked.

"Well, he thinks he looks upsetting," his mother said.

Now Jeff saw why. The operation on the cancer at his jawline mutilated him. In addition, his head was shaved, skull and face red with radiation burns, and his neck had vivid rows of stitching. The part of his face he retained looked wrong, and though he could make himself understood his speech was thick and effortful.

But he smiled, however grotesquely.

"Good to have you home," Jeff said. (Was lying always so easy?)

"Good to be home," his Dad answered. "Thought I'd never get out of that place. Congratulations on getting into Garrett Prep. I'm very proud."

"Thank you."

"Dinner's ready soon," said his mother, coming in with a martini for Dent, a gin-and-tonic for herself.

"Eating with us?" asked Jeff, getting up as his mother sat down.

"Not tonight, Sport," his father said, eyes sparkling as he grasped his drink. "Oh thank God, Carol. What the doctors don't know. . . *Skål*."

"*Skål*."

AFTER DINNER, JEFF put on tie and jacket — wrists poking out of the sleeves — clad his big feet in cordovan brogues made of Corfam (DuPont's synthetic leather that soon vanished from the market) and at 7:00 o'clock was ready to greet his

— *THE HOLY HUGS OF FATHER S.* —

classmates. In this final semester dance lessons had been arranged for twenty 8th graders, and Jeff's family room volunteered as their venue.

Mrs. Adams, the instructor, arrived carrying her portable phonograph and the evening's stack of 78s and 45s and set up in a corner. The book-lined family room was sizable, though not overlarge with so many in it. Jeff's classmates arrived by ones and twos, half boys, half girls, a few mothers staying on to chaperone, the rest darting away, to return in two hours.

Jeff's mother happily told the others that her husband was home from the hospital. "He's fine, he's fine," she assured them.

Outdoors, light from the setting sun filtered through the trees while birds sang an insistent chorus.

Waltzes and foxtrots being the teacher's specialty (and the parents' desire), the girls and boys decorously practiced their box steps—never needed at St. Jude's cafeteria Teen Club dances, whose music was Motown or rock.

But after every three or four *Begin the Beguine*s (fox trot) or *Moon River*s (waltz), Mrs. Adams dropped the needle on the Stones' *(I Can't Get No) Satisfaction* or the Beatles' *Twist and Shout* and the kids happily got down to it. Dancing to *Satisfaction* the boys tended almost to pogo, *pounding, pounding, pounding*, working up a sweat, faces flushed, before resuming due posture and cadence for the *Swan Lake Waltz*.

After Ed Sullivan's TV show of February 9, 1964, Beatlemania swept St. Jude's like bubonic plague, and it never ebbed. Nothing could stop it, despite heroic efforts. Sister Bernadette, the principal, banned all mention of

Beatles and forbade the sharing or bringing to school of Beatles records, posters, paperbacks, bubble-gum cards, fan magazines, wigs or boots. Jeff's 6th-grade teacher, Sister Nathaniel, boomed: "Beetles are *bugs* and bugs should be *stepped* on!"

Jeff's comeback got a laugh: "But, Sister, you had *Frankie*."

He had her there.

Jeff never understood hostility towards the Beatles or rock music generally—all those gorgeous harmonies? But the nuns were aghast at how the unstoppable tide of hormones was making their docile little pupils responsive to—excitable by—R&B and rock. One day, Sister Briana strode to the light switch and flicked off the overheads. Girls' excitement, she explained, was slow to build. But *boys'*? She flicked the lights on, flooding the room with fluorescence.

"Like *that*," she said grimly.

Jeff did the best he could dancing with girls while wishing he had a boy in his arms.

As a challenge Mrs. Adams played the Beatles' *Yesterday*. Hesitant at first, everybody was accurately waltzing to it when Carol made a white-faced appearance. She said something to the instructor and the evening ended a little early.

"I think it was bothering Daddy," she told Jeff.

3.

FATHER SCHMIDT SAID 7:00 a.m. Mass seven days a week. He didn't look or feel well at that hour but, face pasty, eyes hollow, came around the old altar to the new stone table facing the congregation (as newly decreed by the Second Vatican Council) and sped through the liturgy. He was famous for his speedy Masses — beloved for them. Eleven minutes was his record — and an awesome one! — but Vatican II threw a spanner in the works. Instead of rapid-fire Latin — having memorized it phonetically, Father could rattle through it as fast as teeth and tongue permitted, untrammeled by meaning — now he had to make it English, speak as though he meant to be understood by those in front of him.

No more speed records.

Which was a shame. Mass at 7:00 in the morning was no social occasion to show off new hats or outfits, but a workingman's service, attended by those who felt they had no choice in the matter. Exchanging the obscure Latin for the surprising earnestness of the English — *"Peace be with you!"* (could anything sound less Roman Catholic?) — was all very well, but the new Kiss of Peace required people actually to touch one another. Its accompaniment became an instantly conventional clench of lips and teeth. Peace wasn't what Father's 7:00 o'clock faithful were there for.

Often Jeff served as altar boy, bicycling or walking to the church. But face drawn and voice throaty, he was no more an early bird than Father, who would joke about their being a fine pair.

That Saturday as Jeff helped drape vestments over the priest's black shirt and pants, Father said, "Heard about your acceptance to Garrett Prep. Congratulations."

"Thanks, Father."

"And about your Dad coming home. You must be so happy. How's he doing?"

"He's pretty quiet. Letting friends come by and visit, though."

"That's good. Like a ride home later in my new car?"

"I've got my bike."

"Load it in the trunk."

Then they went out and got through Mass smoothly. Jeff seldom made a misstep, never kept Father waiting, shook his four-bell array with a prompt attack. Except on Sunday, there was no sermon, which was good, as preaching wasn't Father's forte.

There were fifteen in the congregation, spread from front to back of a church capacious and handsome without being expensive. The interior was a shed of curved wooden beams upholding a cathedral ceiling of polished wood and hanging lanterns. The front wall was stone, the others of glossy tan cinder block, the windows as yet mere frosted panes. It being Lent, the statues of Mary (stage right) and Joseph (stage left) — not to mention Jesus' rock abdominals on the crucifix—were shrouded in purple, as were the stations of the cross.

After Mass Jeff again turned down the offer of a ride, but Father said he'd swing by later to visit his Dad, even though he knew—everybody knew—Jeff's father wasn't Catholic. Dent was Protestant, if cagey about which denomination he might have been raised in.

Jeff rode home, ate breakfast and visited with his Dad, who his mother said was better today.

Then he got busy. Though barely mid-March, it was a warm day, and he wanted to wash both cars for the first time that year. Finding a chamois and the hose, he went to it.

The Mustang was the 1964½ model his Dad was one of the first to buy, when Mustangs were more rumored than seen. In the two years since, wherever it went it turned heads.

And to soap it down—every line assertive, graceful, classy—was a sensual experience. The car relied for its effect not on chrome or mass, but on proportion and restraint, on how the long hood and short deck worked together, on the confidence of its roofline and wheel openings.

He rinsed it and let it dry while he turned to the car beside it, the 1961 Lincoln Continental. There was a Cadillac up the street whose bullying size and protestations of importance made Jeff wince. The Lincoln? Perfectly proportioned, elegant, sharing with the Mustang an expressive little bump at the collarline as endearing as a bump in a nose. But whereas the Mustang's sides were scooped and sculptural, the Lincoln's were sheer slabs, haughty beneath an understated edging of chrome that rode from headlights to taillights.

Not to mention suicide doors.

Jeff soaped it lovingly, rubbing every corner of its complicated grille, and rinsed it off.

Then he waxed both cars, spreading Turtle Wax over the fenders, rubbing it in, letting it dry and smoothing it away, shining the Mustang's startling bronze paint and the chrome pony galloping across its grille and polishing the Lincoln's black to illimitable depths. *Gorgeous*.

Exchanging the scent of wax for the house's new smell—something to do with his sick Dad upstairs—he found Spray 409 and paper towels to clean the interiors.

He tuned the Lincoln's radio to WINX. *California Dreaming*, just beautiful. The trouble with the interiors was cigarette smoke. Jeff's parents were heavy smokers, two-packs-a-day smokers, so wiping the windows turned Jeff's paper towel as brown as if he were wiping his ass. *Nowhere Man*. Jeff loved the Beatles, but thought *Nowhere Man* a tad preachy. The same sticky brown came off the dashboard, chrome switches and dials, the leather, the wood inlays. *These Boots Are Made for Walking*. All right, by now walking straight down the charts.

Jeff turned to the Mustang and its simpler interior, similarly coated in brown. The headliners were a nightmare to wipe to an approximation of white. *Homeward Bound*. Dent stopped smoking with his diagnosis; too late, of course. Jeff always hated his parents' smoking, and was a pill about it. After every meal came the cigarettes, whose smoke made beelines for his face. *In the Midnight Hour*. As a concession to his complaints his mother or father might showily move an ashtray aside.

Ballad of the Green Berets. Really?

—THE HOLY HUGS OF FATHER S.—

Turning off the radio, Jeff got the vacuum cleaner and, plugging into the carport, swept both cars. And was done, satisfied.

As he finished a car pulled up and a colleague of his Dad's got out. Jeff took him indoors and soon laughter was booming from Dent's bedroom as they reminisced about how any dry day of reporting from The Hill and its closemouthed solons might be redeemed by dropping by the office of Kentucky's junior Senator in late afternoon, when Thruston Morton's tongue was so well oiled as to let inquiring reporters in on anything they might wish to know.

Father Schmidt came by late that morning and visited with Dent, but Jeff, reading in his room, didn't make an appearance.

ON SATURDAY AFTERNOON everybody has better things to do than attend choir practice, but Father didn't know when else to hold it. The week's big practice—it included the men—was scheduled for 2:00 p.m.

Back from the Osbornes', he ate lunch in the rectory kitchen—ham sandwiches he made himself, Mrs. Logan not coming in weekends—then dressed with care, taking the clinging plastic off a dry-cleaned black jacket. Backing the Fury into Teagers Mill Road, he dashed off to church.

Cars were arriving as he drove into the circle and felt a new worry: The short drive barely nudged the needle of the Fury's temperature gauge, and surely it was best to warm up the engine fully? Especially while he was still breaking it in? So he sat revving it, watching the needle jerk its way to the middle of its arc while choristers passed, concern on some faces at the sight of him sitting there.

After this, he decided, he'd take a longer, more roundabout route to church.

His happiest hours then began, walking up the "new" classroom wing to the choir room. Everybody chatted for a few minutes: They'd made it! Even on such a Spring-like Saturday, there they were!

Father raised his voice. "Afternoon, everybody," he said. "Page 207 of your hymnals, please."

Twenty minutes of Gregorian chant always set a mood:

> *In die solemnitatis vestrae, dicit Dominus,*
> *inducam vos in terram fluentem lac et mel. . .*

Nothing so pleased Father as a choir composed of men and boys, notes scraping the bass bottom and soaring to soprano heights. You get there through cooperation and respect, the Lord nudging you along because to Him, too, there's nothing finer than to hear His loving creation reflected in song.

Father was proud of his choir's growing reputation. Not only was it frequently booked for services at the National Shrine, it had a standing engagement—enormously prestigious—for the annual Mass celebrating John F. Kennedy's birthday at St. Matthew's Cathedral. This year's was hardly two months away.

"*Good,*" he said finally, and praised Jeff's and Conor's from-the-diaphragm breathing, which gave such control to their phrasing. Typical of how Father Schmidt taught by encouragement. But he knew the delicacy of boys, the vulnerability they can feel singing in public.

Then they worked on hymns the congregation would

–THE HOLY HUGS OF FATHER S.–

join in on at tomorrow's High Mass. Father was jealous of Protestants' hymns, so much less lugubrious than Catholics', but his choir's impeccable renditions helped pick up the pace.

After an hour they took a break, used the water fountain or restroom and chatted.

"Father, is that your new car? The Fury?"

For a few minutes he talked cubic inches and horsepower, before everybody reassembled and he handed out his mimeographed *Children, Go Where I Send Thee*, a complex Christmas carol from the Black South he'd heard the Seekers sing. If he could get a sense of how it sounded, they'd have plenty of time to perfect it.

He sang it solo—his baritone strong—then assigned the different parts, and began leading them through it. Soon it was sounding well—lively, novel, the boys' faces lighting up as they solved the unfamiliar chromatic lines.

Father Schmidt, pleased, was aware also of a certain disquiet—one he felt more strongly every week.

St. Jude's School having opened with only grades 1 through 3, his first choristers were little boys. He liked them, of course—*loved* them, but not in *that* sense. He recruited men for his choir, too, nor did they pose much temptation, not really, and he gratefully accepted their wives' dinner invitations.

Now something new was happening. The school having added one grade annually—this year's 8th graders having been, as it were, seniors every year—boys he met when they were six, seven, eight years old were 11, 12, 13.

A 12-year-old boy's often more girl than man, but *13*?

They were changing in front of his eyes. Voices were the least of it: Things were beginning to stick out.

Surrounded by meaty new hips, thighs, crotches, shoulders, Father Schmidt was disconcerted and excited. The eyes looking back at him suddenly seemed knowing, adult, full of speculation, making assumptions.

Something about Jeff snagged his attention. He had a way of holding the mimeograph with his fingertips so that—as he told Father—he could feel the paper vibrate from their voices. But today the boy was looking back at him with a mature, aware expression. He supposed having your Dad dying makes a boy grow up overnight.

"Before I dismiss you," Father said, "I've got a big announcement. Monsignor will be talking about it at Mass tomorrow: The parish is being given a great honor, and it includes *you*.

"No, not talking about the JFK birthday Mass. We'll be doing that too, though, rest assured.

"No, even more exciting: The National Liturgical Council is producing a 45-minute movie about the effects of Vatican II. It'll be shown on TV next fall. It's called *We Are Christ,* and the Archbishop's arranged for it to be filmed right here at St. Jude's the week after Easter—just four weeks from now! We'll be in it, and one of the main characters is our own Johnny Capistrano. Johnny, thanks for keeping the secret!

"OK, that's it, thank you very much!"

They dispersed in a buzz of excitement.

4.

THE NEXT DAY Jeff was standing with the choir at High Mass, stage right of the altar. Another warm day, but no one had thought to open the windows. Sometimes the ushers opened them during services, taking a pole from window to window to push up the sashes, get a cross breeze going, but today no one did it and, his surplice heavy on him, Jeff felt warm and hemmed in as High Mass made its stately progress.

The church was crowded. People loved St. Jude's sung High Mass, despite what Father Schmidt saw (or heard) as its glaring drawback: The fact that Monsignor was so entirely tone deaf.

Father marveled at his complete inability to carry a tune or find a rhythm, but Monsignor professed to be unbothered. "I am as God made me," he'd say. "If I'm good enough for Him..."

But it pained the ear, hurt afresh every time he droned off-key, *"The grace of our Lord Jesus Christ, and the love of God, and the fellowship of the Holy Spirit be with you all."* Like dragging chalk across a blackboard. In Latin it at least had seemed allusive, atavistic, mystical— "*Gràtia Dòmini nostrì Jesu Christi, et càritas Dei, et communicàtio Sancti Spiritus sit cum òmnibus vobis"* —but the new liturgy's English made it *excruciating*. People wondered if it was this that yet kept him from becoming a bishop.

Father Schmidt suspected Monsignor's easy acceptance of his voice concealed shame he could do no better, and that that shame helped explain his own presence in the parish.

The homily provided a respite; Monsignor was known as a preacher. The dark Friday Kennedy was shot—that dreadful day that kicked the legs out from under the country—he said a special Mass for the President's soul before the body was back in Washington. St. Jude's thronged with weeping parishioners, he spoke practically off the cuff, eloquently and feelingly, then had a publicist's presence of mind to type up his sermon and get it to the Washington *Post*, which printed it the next day. Monsignor hoped it comforted people.

Today, garbed in rich purple mourning vestments, part of the Catholic theatre of Lent, he spoke of how Vatican II was bringing the liturgy closer to the faithful, and smoothly segued to the movie, telling his gratified congregation that it was to star in *We Are Christ*.

"Mass will be filmed right here with any of you who wish to participate attending. The filmmakers will also follow four young parishioners as they experience the new liturgy in their daily lives.

"This movie's a signal honor for St. Jude's—a terrific compliment to us and a testament to your faith. Going to be exciting!"

The choir sang the Offertory while bells rang, coins

chinked and envelopes piled up amidst clicks from the censer, clouds of incense wafting upwards. Meanwhile Jeff's vision splintered—and he fainted, fortunately breaking his fall by dropping onto boys in front.

"*Oh!*" went the cry, and even Monsignor ceased his caterwauling but, leaping forward, Father Schmidt picked Jeff up and carried him out the side door, pushed open by Conor scrambling ahead. Father felt like St. Christopher, or St. Peter at the descent from the cross. Jeff weighed some 135 lbs., but Father knew he could carry him all day long.

Behind them, Monsignor resumed his monotone.

Outdoors, along the convent driveway, cooler air on his face, Jeff revived immediately. Setting him down on the curbing, Father asked Conor to see if Dr. Alban was in his regular pew.

"I don't need a doctor," Jeff protested, getting to his feet. "I'm OK. Just got too hot. I'll go find my mother."

"Good," said Father.

Carol was relieved when Jeff slipped into the last pew beside her, but hadn't been too worried, especially after seeing Father come back indoors. People fainted at Mass sometimes, just as it also appeared to provoke epileptic fits.

But they skipped the bake sale that followed High Mass, though going on to the newsstand off Georgia Avenue to buy the weighty Sunday *New York Times* for Dent.

The house they returned to smelled of sickness—of cancer, Jeff supposed. Illness pervaded every corner, for all that Dent stayed in his bedroom, generally with the door closed. Shifts of nurses operated out of the upstairs guest room.

Jeff went up to see his Dad, who lay with his head

turned to the greenery outdoors, too preoccupied to take in his apology for not getting anything at the bake sale. But the nurse smiled at him.

Later Jeff brought in a pair of Dent's colleagues and his Dad perked up. He fielded questions about when he might return to the office and reminisced about the time they took a room next to the suite where the Democratic National Committee was writing its 1960 party platform and discussing candidates. Putting their ears to the wall, they caught some of the gossip, then made a closer approach by taking off a grille and crawling into a duct.

5.

TUESDAY, JEFF WALKED to church in fog and slowly encroaching daylight to serve early Mass, only to find a white horse grazing beneath St. Jude's windows.

He and the horse looked at each other. A symbolic horse, he wondered? An allegorical horse? No, just a hungry horse. He told Father, who phoned the horse farm about its runaway.

Perhaps it had heard about the horse farm's being sold?

Encountering a horse was unusual, but not as unusual as the day school didn't open because there were no nuns. Children wandered the blacktop, lost, while others knocked and knocked on the convent door.

The sisters returned about 9:30, having spent the night in jail.

Sister Madonna told Jeff's class the story. It was the spring of 1964, and all the sisters had gone Downtown after school the day before to demonstrate for the Civil Rights Act then before Congress.

The demonstration was coming to a peaceful end when a police captain arrived and yelled, *"GET THESE*

NIGGERLOVERS OUT OF HERE!"

"Once we heard that," said Sister Madonna, eyes flashing, "we weren't going *anywhere*."

Instead, she and her fellow demonstrators sat down on Pennsylvania Avenue and were duly carted off to jail. Fortunately, no charges were laid and, the Archbishop being outspoken in favor of civil rights, their arrests led to no repercussions.

Today, instead of unlocking the choir room as he usually did after Mass so Jeff could read until class started, Father Schmidt suggested breakfast out, his treat.

"Get you back in plenty of time," he assured him.

The Fury dashed them to the Hot Shoppe at Wheaton Plaza, and soon they were facing stacks of pancakes.

Hot Shoppes were a venture of J.W. Marriott's before he entered the hotel business. Dent once interviewed Marriott in the library of his Bethesda mansion and amused himself by counting every book in it: 24. A grand total of 24 books! In the evening teenagers circled the restaurant for hours on end, revving their engines at one another, but this morning it was sunny and cheerful, busy with breakfasters.

"Father," Jeff asked, "how did you know you had a vocation?"

Father took it in stride, chewing and swallowing before he answered.

"Well, for me, I didn't *know,* but it was in the back of my mind early as grade school. Went to public high school, then on to a Catholic college—Villanova—where I discerned my vocation clearly.

"Why? Do you think you might have one?"

"I don't know."

—THE HOLY HUGS OF FATHER S.—

"If you do, you'll discern it. You'll know."

They ate silently for a minute.

"How's your father doing?"

"Better, I think."

"Good. You know, Jeff, if you ever want to talk about him, or anything at all, you can always call me. Just call the rectory, day or night, or leave a note in my box in Sister Bernadette's office."

"Thank you, Father," said Jeff, his eyes filling. Father's filled sympathetically.

"Want anything else?"

"No, thanks, I'm full. But thank you."

Father got the check and they headed to St. Jude's. Getting out of the Fury in the circle as children gathered for class, Jeff greeted his friends with the modesty becoming a favorite.

WHEN DR. WHITE visited his patient that morning, he assured Carol that things were progressing. No one articulated towards what goal things were progressing, but she thought she could figure it out, especially when he added, "If—forgive me, but I know you belong to St. Jude's—if you're thinking in terms of Extreme Unction—sorry, Last Rites they call it now? Well, about any time, Mrs. Osborne."

"Dent's not Catholic."

"Ah," said the doctor. "That I did not know."

It was fortunate that Jeff's Dad worked for ORBS Magazine, because there was never a company more generous to its employees.

Dent loved his colleague's story about spending weeks

cruising the Pacific embedded with the crew of the Navy's newest aircraft carrier. The expense account he submitted included a generous provision for taxicabs. An alert beancounter flagging the anomaly, the reporter countered by telegram, "Longest damn ship you ever saw," and was recompensed in full.

ORBS's generosity meant round-the-clock nurses for Dent, which made things easier.

The week passed in suspense. The doctor came daily, professional and unflappable, and the nurses changed shifts with exaggerated good cheer, but Dent lay in his crank-up bed, head turned to the windows, ignoring TV and radio even during the news.

ON SATURDAY, Carol assuring him the noise wouldn't disturb his Dad—rather, he'd enjoy it—Jeff mowed the lawn. Grass covered three quarters of an acre, so it was a substantial undertaking. He yanked the Toro alive and set off and back again, pushing it down and back, down and back, attentive as he needed to be but his mind free to wander.

He fantasized that he and his friend Conor—he really liked Conor—were driving a 1956 Thunderbird with a porthole in the roofline across the country; a fantasy derived from *Route 66*, the TV show, but one Jeff found absorbing nonetheless. What color was their T-bird? White? Turquoise? He couldn't decide, then realized it was a convertible; no porthole after all.

Conor was bright, good-looking, led their playground gang and served as campaign manager when Jeff was elected class president. His family belonged to the same swim club as Jeff's, and it was Conor who informed him that one could use the restroom in the men's locker room, then, by marching out the long way, usually see naked men.

The previous summer the boys one day left the pool to go to Conor's house, where no one was home. Jeff was nervous and excited about what Conor (or even himself) might have in mind, but inevitably a sibling who was supposed to be elsewhere was home instead and curious about what they were up to.

Finished mowing, he clipped, collected $2 from his mother and cut the smell of sickness by stirring up a pitcher of lemonade. He carried a glass of it in to his Dad, who, rallying a little, reminisced about Colorado.

Dent Osborne was promoted to managing editor of the Grand Junction *Daily Sentinel*—same job Dalton Trumbo once held, he always maintained—after its owner accepted an appointment to the U.S. Senate and his son took over the publishing reins.

But when the pressmen walked out, the son demanded that everybody help break the strike and take a loyalty oath to himself. The McCarthy era at its peak—Dalton Trumbo himself blacklisted by Hollywood—Jeff's Dad, with a wife and two sons to support, and who felt a little compromised anyway because, though technically he hadn't crossed the picket line, he'd continued his habit of entering the premises from the rear, stood up and in a voice whose tremulousness he regretted but couldn't control, announced, "I quit."

"So foolish," he told Jeff, "except it turned out to be the best move I ever made." A *Sentinel* colleague who was a stringer for ORBS recommended him to his editors there,

Dent followed his clippings to New York, underwent a grueling round of interviews and was hired.

"That's when we went to Disneyland?" asked Jeff.

"That's when we went to Disneyland. Your grandmother rented a cottage at Laguna Beach and while we were there, waiting for ORBS to hire me, we visited Disneyland. It had only opened a few months earlier. Surprised you remember. You were three years old—three and a half?"

"I remember *vividly*," Jeff told him. "The teacups? The flying Dumbos? The *Mark Twain* and the railroad? And Autopia! Oh, the tantrum I threw when they wouldn't let me drive! Three years old."

His father chuckled, sighed and drifted off.

For dinner Carol fixed one of her standbys, *porcupines*, ground-beef meatballs rolled in rice and baked with tomatoes. Eating with her at the kitchen table, Jeff pretended not to listen when the nurse called the doctor about adjusting the morphine.

Later Jeff kissed his parents goodnight and went to bed. Tonight he read some Evelyn Waugh—his Dad's favorite, *Scoop*—before snapping off the light to listen on his Sony transistor radio to WWDC's Steve Allison greet a pair of frequent guests from the Mattachine Society. As usual they declared how natural and normal homosexuality is.

Though glad to hear it, Jeff thought it an ugly word to contend with—it sounded like a deliberately affronting concoction; he preferred the lighter *gay* they sometimes used, nor had he any settled objections to *queer*. He could see them, earnest in suits and ties, and see also the scandalized diners in the steakhouse from which the show broadcast, turning to their filets while in his mildly adversarial way Allison drew out his guests.

Finally Jeff switched off the radio, turned over and assaulted his mattress to images of those friends he most desired. He imagined sharing a tent with Conor out in the trees — a feasible fantasy, actually! — at nightfall zipping it shut and taking off his shirt, glimpsing Conor taking off *his*, then taking off shoes, socks, pants, while seeing Conor do the same, then turning to him and —

He ejaculated, and soon fell asleep.

6.

NEXT DAY—PALM SUNDAY—before leaving for Mass, Carol called to her husband from the doorway.

"We'll bring home the *Times* and something from the bake sale. Anything you'd especially like?"

Seeming to smile, Dent uttered what she heard as Boston cream pie.

"We'll get one if they have it," she assured him, though she worried: Boston cream pies were donated irregularly by one particular, if unknown, parishioner.

They took the Lincoln, the perfect go-to-meeting vehicle, bolstering her self-esteem even as her husband lay ill. But he seemed better today.

The choir was in good voice at High Mass and, windows open, there was a delicious breeze through the church.

In the choir room afterwards, Father Schmidt asked, "How's your Dad, Jeff?"

"Better, thanks, Father. He's better this weekend."

"OK if I come by to visit?"

"Sure," Jeff told him, tearing off his surplice and hurrying after his fellows to the cafeteria.

There, tables arranged in a grand square groaned under home-baked goods. There were coffee cakes, layer cakes, sheet cakes, pies, cookies, muffins, turnovers, Danishes, breads of every kind, everything wrapped in foil, waxed paper or plastic.

Jeff went rapidly along, looking for a Boston cream pie, but it was his mother across the tabletops who found it. He saw her do it — spot that day's sole exemplar, and reach for it even as another woman reached for it, too. Making a moue of appeal, Carol shot out her other arm, grabbed it and made off with it.

"You found it!"

"The things I do. Choir sounded lovely today, honey."

"Thanks."

She paid — the cake a pricey $4 — and spoke to ladies in passing — "How's your husband?" "Better, thanks" — as they went out to the hall and into the parking lot. Getting away from church after Mass had its own ceremonial, and of course before going home they had to dash to the newsstand for the *Times*.

But finally they were turning under Storybook Forest's fresh green canopy — glossily reflected in the car's hood, whose rifle-sight ornament aimed them accurately home while the Supremes sang *Baby Love*.

Carol pulled into the driveway beside the Mustang. Jeff carried the newspaper and cake through the front door — and stopped.

Something was different. Changed.

The nurse came to the top of the stairs. His mother ran up from behind him to the bedroom, and there found her husband's body already composed in a simulacrum of peace, eyes and mouth closed, hands clasping each other on top of the coverlet.

"I'm so sorry, Mrs. Osborne," said the nurse. "It was very peaceful."

"When?"

"Eleven-thirty. You'd just left. I think he waited until you were gone. I called Dr. White, he'll pronounce him."

Carol didn't know what to do. Everything necessary was in course of being done, leaving her free to *feel*, but she didn't want to *feel*, she wanted something to *do*. Her husband of 23 years lay before her, his body suddenly irrelevant. But she stepped forward to touch and kiss his hands and forehead, bending over to murmur. She had no tears. She'd already wept those tears.

Jeff did have tears, a flood of them, so scalding he almost tripped in turning around and going downstairs. He locked his door.

The doctor arrived, put a stethoscope to Dent's chest, nodded, sadly filled out a document and left chewing a slice of Boston cream pie.

Arrangements having been made with Pumphrey's, and the nurse kindly telephoning them, their black Econoline van turned into the driveway and two big men in dark suits brought a litter indoors. Jeff — dry-eyed now — came in and watched them lay it on the other bed, wrap the body in a blanket, transfer it, then heave the litter through the doorway, down the stairs (keeping it remarkably level) and out to the van.

At his mother's suggestion Jeff followed with slices of Boston cream pie on paper plates with plastic forks and paper napkins.

None of the neighbors appeared to be watching, which was some consolation.

—THE HOLY HUGS OF FATHER S.—

A blue Fury pulled up behind the Econoline, then backed out again and parked on the street. Father Schmidt got out and made the sign of the cross at the van and placed his hand on the roof. The driver looked steadily at him and, at a mutually agreeable moment, wiped his mouth, put down his plate and drove off.

Father Schmidt found Carol and Jeff at the door and embraced them both, Carol bursting into tears at last.

Somehow they moved upstairs and sat down, and Jeff fetched slices of cake for everybody, not omitting one for the nurse clearing up in the bedroom. She'd already stripped the bed and cranked it flat, to be picked up later. The windows open, no trace or taint of sickness remained.

"So good," said Father Schmidt, chewing.

"His favorite," sobbed Carol.

The taste of sponge, cream and chocolate comforted Jeff, too, though he scoffed at himself.

Father held Carol through a crying jag. But she had phone calls to make, so finally disengaged from him. "Lately from Jeff it's just been Father Schmidt *this*, Father Schmidt *that*, Father. Thank you so much."

She sat down at the kitchen phone. A Cleveland Park friend said she'd be out within the hour to stay the night. As a neighbor lady came upstairs Carol hung up and burst into tears again.

Father Schmidt asked Jeff, "Want to get out of here?"

"Yes!"

It was fine with Carol. Driving out from under the trees, they headed to McDonald's in Glenmont. Jeff took Father's money to the window for cheeseburgers, fries and milk shakes. There being no seating area, they ate in the car. Little was said; nothing about Jeff's father's death.

Finished, Jeff put their trash into a receptacle.

"Come on," said Father. "Let's see some countryside."

For an hour Jeff swayed in his seat as, beneath a sky of full-bodied blue, Father Schmidt gunned the Fury past horse pastures and white fences, radio turned up loud: *Day Tripper, Uptight (Everything's Alright), 19th Nervous Breakdown.*

He never turned to look at Jeff, according him privacy as the car accelerated into curves or overtook slower vehicles.

But as, in his peripheral vision, he saw him settle down, become attentive to the landscape, Father turned around and headed back to the house.

When they arrived at Trent Lane—dread building inside Jeff at every turning in Storybook Forest—they found cars massed in front of the house as though for Sunday barbecue.

"If you want," said Father, "I could ask your mom if you can stay at the rectory tonight? Plenty of room. Get you out of her hair."

"Yes, Father, *please*. Thank you."

"Need anything?"

"Don't think so."

Leaving the radio on *(Barbara Ann, Daydream)*, Father stepped indoors.

When he emerged with Carol's permission, he'd also volunteered to meet Jeff's brother's flight from California the next morning.

Getting in the car, he asked, "Do you like Kentucky Fried Chicken?"

"Sure."

"Let's get a bucket. But first I'd like to stop off at the

new rectory, check the progress."

It was all but finished, a handsome, well-proportioned brick house of size and dignity. St. Jude's was prospering, and though Monsignor insisted on building church, school and convent first, he knew it was time to raise a fine rectory.

Father used his key to open the rear double doors to a terrazzo-floored foyer that continued to the front double doors.

"Wow," said Jeff.

"Here's our living room," Father said, leading him into it.

"Wow," Jeff said again.

"Dining room, with another fireplace. Pantry. Kitchen. Mudroom. Housekeeper's room—Mrs. Logan's going to live in. A kind of family room. Monsignor's office, mine over here, and a spare."

Everything was roomy, bright and expensively outfitted. Already a certain amount of furniture sat about, delivered from Woodward & Lothrop or Hecht's and still wrapped in plastic or brown paper.

"Let's see the upstairs," said Father, taking the broad carpeted steps two at a time. "Library, chapel, four suites."

"Four? Are you adding priests?"

"Or for guests. Here's mine."

He led Jeff into a corner study that on one side overlooked playground, church and school, on the other the new soccer field abutting Wheaton Regional Park's 500 forested acres. Jeff peered into the dressing room and bathroom, and in the bedroom stood beside Father regarding the new twin mattress.

"What do you think of the color?" Father asked of his

pale yellow walls. "Only walls in the house that aren't off-white."

"Nice."

"Can't wait to make the move. Well, just wanted to check up."

"It's really nice, Father—like a hotel suite."

They drove to Four Corners to pick up chicken, then to the old rectory. Jeff had never been inside. It reminded him of his family's old house a few blocks away, though furnished more like a men's club in leather couches and chairs.

"Let's bring it in here," Father called. Jeff carried the chicken to the Chesterfield sofa in front of the living-room TV. "What do you want to drink? Coke? Beer?"

"*Beer?*"

"Why not?"

"Coke's fine, Father. Is Monsignor here?"

"Sunday night? *Kidding?* Stays over at his sister's in Potomac. Drumstick? Breast?"

Father Schmidt had two quick beers while speaking fondly of the priest who helped him discern *his* vocation.

The doorbell rang and Father took his drumstick with him to answer it. It was a bake-sale lady with a leftover cake.

"I'll cut up that cake later. Sure you don't want a beer?"

"Maybe I'll try one."

"Good man."

"My grandfather used to give me sips. I liked them."

Jeff gripped his Budweiser, trying to drink it as if he drank beer every day.

"Like it?"

"Yes."

— *THE HOLY HUGS OF FATHER S.* —

They watched one of the eclectic offerings of Washington's new channel 20: bullfights from Mexico City with commentary by the American matador Sidney Franklin. In his effeminate voice, Franklin expertly described the bulls and the bullfighters' moves—"another veronica." Jeff was mesmerized by silk-hipped toreadors gracefully dispatching bull after bull.

"Another beer?"

Before answering Jeff took stock of how he felt: somehow enlarged, his troubles at a distance. But he knew they could be put at a greater distance still.

"Sure, please," he said.

As they watched TV, Father Schmidt laid an arm across the boy's shoulder. Yawning, he jokingly clapped that hand to his mouth, throttling Jeff in the process. They laughed.

Jeff steadied his dizziness by anchoring himself against the priest. Father kissed his temple, and under his breath intoned a prayer in Latin.

Later Jeff woke up in the guest room, which had a double bed and its own color TV. Father Schmidt lying beside him, they watched Ed Sullivan, enjoying his guests Stiller & Meara and snapping to attention (Father especially) at the Archdiocesan Chorus of New York's singing *Soon I Will Be Done* (Father said he preferred Mahalia Jackson's version).

Jeff yawned. He wanted nothing but to go back to sleep.

"Let me help," said Father Schmidt, tousling Jeff's hair and undoing his shirt buttons. His glasses off, Father's expression was as ecstatic as at choir practice. "Do you know how bodies work? Here, I'll show you."

Jeff was suddenly wide awake.

7.

FORTUNATELY THEY WOKE up in time for early Mass, by 7:30 were on their way to Dulles, munching on the toast-and-honey Father thought to bring.

The priest had never felt so alive. He knew he'd sinned, but doubted that something so much fun and accomplished without coercion, or at least violence—not more than disregarding Jeff's "Pull out! Pull out, *please!*"— could be mortal sin, and he knew from seminary that mortal sin allows no such doubt, but requires *certainty*. The sin Father was guilty of therefore being venial, he'd said Mass without a qualm.

Jeff beside him, at University Boulevard Father sped the Fury onto the Beltway, enjoyed flying through the treetops and across the Potomac. After a half decade's construction, the Capital Beltway had opened two years earlier. The concrete columns of the overpasses, poured first, taunted Father for years until Rustoleum-orange beams were finally hoisted up to span them. Now he was up there, zipping along.

He couldn't quite believe the night just past. Knock-

—THE HOLY HUGS OF FATHER S.—

knock-knocking at heaven's door, *opening* it—breaking *through*—he'd found more wonderful sensations of release than he'd ever felt before. Murmuring, "Your wife will be glad you know these things," his exertions led him to a deep sleep, arms locked around Jeff. In taking his pleasure with him, Father rejoiced in possessing the vocation that let him minister to a grieving boy.

Meanwhile, in contrast to Father, who was chattier than usual, pointing out cars they passed, returning time and again to the story of his vocation, Jeff was quiet. He'd already used the toilet twice that morning, and needed it again.

He was very far away. He'd been drunk, until he wasn't really drunk any longer, but he knew he was betrayed—betrayed by his priest, but also by his own body, its excitement and willingness to help feed that excitement by doing things it never did before. He was angry at himself.

Father reached over to cup his near knee. Jeff shook the hand off.

Exiting the Beltway and crossing farmland amidst virtually no traffic, they pulled up to Eero Saarinen's soaring terminal to meet the redeye from San Francisco.

Dulles Airport was still new and woefully underused. Jeff couldn't view its billowing glass without emotion; he'd seen his Dad off or met him there a dozen times, and didn't know a more glamorous structure. Seldom had he seen any planes, though. Sometimes he'd see one take off or land in what might have been the next county; elevated buses whisked passengers between terminal and aircraft.

Arrivals were handled on the ground floor, where, right on time, Ron emerged, smiling broadly when he saw Jeff, before frowning in grief. He was 19, an English major who'd last been home at Christmas. If he was surprised to see Father Schmidt—their family not being much for socializing with priests or nuns—he kept it to himself.

As they got to the baggage carousel he asked, "How's Mother doing?"

"All right," said Jeff. "In some ways it might be a relief."

"Was it that bad?"

"Pretty bad," said Jeff. "Excuse me."

"I'll go with you."

Leaving Father, they went to the nearest men's room, where, to Ron's surprise—knowing his brother's shyness regarding bodily functions—Jeff entered a stall. To his further surprise, he immediately heard toilet paper being unrolled, swaths of it, then more, a belt buckled and finally a flush.

When he came out, Jeff appeared to be moving tentatively.

"You OK, little brother?"

"Fine."

Jeff indeed felt better, having wiped up that mess still sliding down inside him that felt as if his guts were falling out. But at the car Ron saw how gingerly he sat down in the backseat and said, "Sure no one's been tanning your backside, little brother?"

"Did they give you breakfast on the plane?" asked Father Schmidt.

MONSIGNOR BRANNICK scheduled Dent's funeral for Wednesday. He would preside over a Vigil at Pumphrey's the night before.

For all that Dent didn't belong to the Church, he was to

have a Catholic funeral because he was, or had been, a catechumen—that is, someone intending to convert. For months, Carol accompanied him to the rectory to receive instruction from Monsignor—sessions Dent enjoyed, for jousting with Monsignor on points of doctrine was not unlike interviewing Nixon or JFK.

Monsignor cheerily told him he was all in favor of conversions. "It's never too late," he said. "Until it is."

But Dent ended the sessions after discovering what he took to be Monsignor's vein of insincerity. They were discussing that crucial moment of the Mass when bread is transubstantiated into the Body of Christ, wine into His Blood. Dent protested that he couldn't believe in such out-and-out magic.

"Putting that aside," said Monsignor with a wave of his hand, and for Dent that was that.

But Monsignor looked past the unconsummated conversion so that Dent's soul might have the benefit of a requiem Mass.

These were days of misery for Jeff, for all that he was out of school. Visitors kept the house crowded, Ron thanking them for their covered dishes and deploying his considerable charm to put them at their ease. His mother just wanted to curl up into a ball in her bedroom but, with Ron's help, got through the ordeal of agreeing with everybody that Dent was at peace at last.

Jeff mostly stayed in his room, and rebelled outright against attending the Vigil, which involved a crowd of strangers saying the rosary in front of the casket. But his mother didn't make him go.

The next day was beautiful. Carol lingered outdoors to enjoy its mildness before getting in the Lincoln. Ron drove them to church. It was a smooth operation, she and her sons assembling with friends, neighbors, some local cousins and some of her husband's colleagues, along with St. Jude's students from third grade on up. This was parish custom; Jeff had attended a dozen funerals with his classmates, but never before for somebody he'd actually known. The choir performed, even half the men showing up on a weekday. Father Schmidt threw himself into leading it.

But Jeff was hollow-eyed, a wraith standing up or kneeling or sitting down only because his brother's hand guided his wrist, wishing he were anyplace else on Earth, and feeling everybody staring. He held on to the pew with a white-knuckled grip so as not to faint or float away.

Burial was in the countryside at a cemetery transformed from horse pastures to meadows of flat headstones. Afterwards everybody trudged to their cars with a sense of accomplishment. Carol having said she didn't think she could endure having people to the house, relations hosted a reception at the Olney Inn, not far away, and she got through it all right, though she drank too much.

WAKING UP LATE the next morning with a headache, the house empty but for her children, Carol took her hair of the dog out to the patio.

She loved sitting out there. Even in the dead of winter, her husband in the hospital, she used to pull on his thickest winter coat and carry her gin and cigarettes outdoors to sit peering into the trees as the sun fell behind them. Now, the day balmy and beautiful, a cardigan sufficed.

Jeff came out and sat down beside her.

"How are you doing, honey?" she asked, tapping her Kent into an ashtray.

"Mother, there's something I have to tell you."

"What's that?" Her tone conveyed that, whatever it was, she didn't care to hear it, not today, a fresh widow (how she despised the word!) grappling with more than she could be expected to cope with.

"Father Schmidt did something I didn't like."

"What did he do?" She sipped her drink.

"I can't tell you, Mother, but I didn't like it."

"What was it, honey?"

"I can't tell you."

"Jeff, you have to get used to the idea that you're not alone on Planet Earth. Other people who have different ways of doing things live here, too, with every right—"

"I really didn't like it, but he made me." He heard his own lie. He'd liked some of it, and joined in, until he didn't.

She set her glass down with an exasperated chink and lifted her cigarette.

"If I don't know what he did, I can't do anything about it, can I?"

"No, I guess not," Jeff said.

"Look, honey, we have a death in the family, and this I can tell you for sure: *No one* knows how to behave around death."

"No, I guess not," Jeff repeated, and went back inside the house as, with a sucking sound, Carol took the cigarette from her lips and brought the glass up to them.

8.

AT THE PARISH-PRIEST level Good Friday, the most solemn of Holy Days, is a land-office day for hearing confessions. St. Jude's scheduled Confession from 12:00 noon to 5:00 p.m., accommodating those parishioners who, tracking Jesus' time on the cross, refused to speak between noon and 3:00.

Hearing confessions, Father Schmidt rued, is less amusing than one might hope. Sins tend to the routine and boring, and the drama surrounding their disclosure gets old fast. Father found confessions the most tedious part of the job.

Monsignor Brannick, who would help out for the first few hours, beat Father to church, parking the Grand Prix in the circle while Father warmed up the Fury by taking a longer way. Inside, Monsignor flipped the switches that lit green lights above both confessionals' side compartments.

Parishioners were already lined up and waiting, but before the priests started with them, Father heard Monsignor's confession, and Monsignor his, turning green lights red.

—THE HOLY HUGS OF FATHER S.—

Monsignor's was quick—a point of pride with him, parishioners waiting—but Father Schmidt's turned out to take a while.

"Father, how many times?"

"Three times. Three ejaculations."

Monsignor—*shocked*—peered through the screen. All that either could see of the other were glasses flashing this way and that.

"Did you use force?"

"Oh no!"

"Was there penetration?"

"A little."

"Oh, Father Schmidt. What happened? Did you lose control?"

"I wanted to comfort him, and one thing led to another."

"Disappointed in you. And you didn't think to confess earlier? You've been saying Mass all week? This is mortal sin."

"Is it really? *Mortal* sin? I sincerely didn't think so. He was in *such* need of comforting, his father dead and—"

"Father, you're equivocating. This is a serious matter. We run a school here. We work with *children*."

"I'm sorry, Monsignor."

"Don't let it happen again—not *ever*. One hundred Hail Marys, one hundred Our Fathers."

Father Schmidt was surprised Monsignor would make such a big deal of it. Having been his confessor for seven years, he happened to know all about Monsignor's recurring little-girl fantasies—knew, too, about the one time he did something he shouldn't have (Father had sternly assigned ten Hail Marys, ten Our Fathers). Surely he could have been less harsh?

Kneeling at the communion rail, Father started rattling through his repentance as fast as he could, but had so many prayers to get through that those waiting at his confessional began to exchange looks of surmise, even to leave his line and cross the nave to Monsignor's. And the penitents steadily coming forward to offer up Monsignor's signature three Hail Marys, two Our Fathers gave Father curious sidewise glances as he labored through *his* penance.

But finally he stood up and opened his box for business. Absolved and pure, his record wiped clean, he was determined to sin no more.

Monsignor stayed longer than planned that afternoon, trying to catch up, but eventually left Father to it and went home.

9.

WHEN FATHER SCHMIDT finally got home, bone-tired, he found Mrs. Logan's note:

> St. Pat's called, wants to see Fr. Schmidt "earliest convenience" Sat.

Father frowned. Surely Holy Saturday was an odd day to be summoned downtown?

He told Monsignor about it during a commercial in *The Man from U.N.C.L.E.*, to which Monsignor was devoted, intrigued by what parishioners who worked for certain Government agencies insisted about every episode's screen acknowledging *"the cooperation of the United Network Command for Law Enforcement"* — that the show was as authentic as *The F.B.I.*

"Oh, ah? Downtown?" asked Monsignor. "What about?"

"No idea."

"I'm sure you'll be fine."

Father Schmidt drove in the next morning after Mass and a good breakfast.

He'd met Archbishop O'Boyle several times, of course, usually in the company of the Archbishop's good friend Monsignor Brannick. On consideration, he thought the summons probably concerned May 29's JFK birthday Mass. Always there were decisions to be made about the specific program. Father was open to suggestions.

There was the possibility, too—if an outside one—that the Archbishop wished to discuss *We Are Christ*. Easter Sunday night—the very next evening—the production team was moving into the new Howard Johnson's Motor Lodge on Georgia Avenue, and on Monday morning would begin filming the various strands of its story.

Father knew from the script that camera crews were to follow four young parishioners living their daily lives as enriched by Vatican II. These narratives would flow around the film's centerpiece, to be filmed the following Saturday: a Mass at St. Jude's (low Mass, but the choir participating) that would demonstrate the changes Vatican II wrought, *viz.*, Monsignor, facing his congregation, would officiate in English, not Latin.

Father Schmidt was disappointed that they weren't filming High Mass—surely more cinematic?—but Monsignor Brannick claimed High Mass to be somewhat antithetical to the spirit of Vatican II. Father wondered if the real reason weren't Monsignor's screechiness, but if so he had the solution: overdub him with *his* voice. He knew it could be done, and surely it would improve the film.

Possibly the Archbishop was way ahead of him? Hence his summons?

If not, might he lobby him about it?

Except an auxiliary priest has to be careful about lobbying an Archbishop, particularly one on the verge—so the grapevine insisted — of being named to the College of Cardinals.

Archbishop O'Boyle lived in the rectory of St. Patrick's, Washington's mother parish not far from the White House. Parking on 10th Street, Father made for the English Gothic stone rectory and, tripping up the front steps, rang. A nun in a wimple like a miniature A-frame ski chalet opened the door to a foyer dark as a cave, lit by one sole lamp with a parchment shade.

"Good morning, Sister, Father Schmidt to see the Archbishop."

"Won't you please take a seat, Father?"

He did so, choosing a red-velvet chair beside a window draped with red velvet, and looked around at framed views of martyrdom.

At last he felt a glimmering of disquiet.

The Archbishop's secretary, an up-and-comer of the sort Father personally detested — some good-looking rich kid, glib and ambitious — came in a few minutes later. The younger priest somehow carried off his black frock and white collar stylishly. He was from New York, probably (Father thought darkly) one of Nellie Spellman's coterie.

"Father Schmidt, good of you to come in on such short notice."

"Not at all. Always happy to see His Grace."

"Yes, well, His Grace asked me to see you in his place, Father." He said this while escorting Father Schmidt to his own somewhat brighter office. "The Archbishop's extremely busy — Holy Saturday, you can imagine! — so I'm afraid you're stuck with me. But he wanted to move quickly."

Father Schmidt took the chair indicated, while the

younger priest sat behind the desk. Conspicuously closed were the double doors to the Archbishop's own sanctum, and they stayed closed.

"I'll get right to it, Father. I'm delighted to tell you you're being given a parish of your own at long last: St. Datian's, in Bullnose, Maryland, down in St. Mary's County. Congratulations!"

Father Schmidt's mouth worked, he was so surprised and dismayed.

"*St. Mary's County?*"

St. Mary's County was the Archdiocese's farthest-flung outpost, located at the southernmost tip of the poverty-stricken peninsula jutting into Chesapeake Bay.

"Don't need to tell you how precious St. Mary's is to us as the cradle of the Church in America? The *Ark* and the *Dove* brought the first Catholic colonists in 1634. Landed quite near St. Datian's, in fact. Imagine that."

"But Father—"

"Off the beaten track these days, but the Archbishop knows you'll come to love it."

Monsignor told! thought Father Schmidt: *Monsignor told!*

"When do I—?"

"You're to stay at St. Jude's through this week only, Father. We know it's too late to do anything about the film schedule, so you're to commence your pastoral duties at St. Datian's on Monday, April 18. We wish you every success."

"But what about the JFK birthday Mass next month?"

"Your successor at St. Abigail's has whipped those girls into a choir second only to your own. So sweet sounding. It should work out very well."

"Are you sure I can't step in to see the Archbishop for

two minutes?"

"Sorry, no."

Stunned, Father Schmidt angrily worked to his feet, lenses flashing over the flushed planes of his face.

"What have we come to," he asked, "when the seal of the confessional means *nothing?*"

"Father," said the younger priest, politely and dismissively.

10.

MONSIGNOR BRANNICK insisted it didn't seem precipitous to *him*.

"*Late*, if anything. You've been my auxiliary seven years! High time you got your reward."

He also professed satisfaction that Father would know a priest's greatest joy: caring for a flock of his own. But for Father Schmidt it was a bitter countdown to exile — *again*.

Monsignor chose High Mass the next morning — Easter Sunday, Lenten shrouds at last off the statues, his vestments gold, the church resplendent and full of flowers — to announce "news sad for me personally and for the parish, but *joyful* for Father Schmidt": Promoted to the birthplace of the Church in America!

Father Schmidt, standing in front of his choir, fielded the murmurs of dismay this elicited by nodding left and right with an expression he didn't mean to look so furtive. After Mass well-wishers thronged him.

Later he drove out to the Osbornes. Since Monsignor would sleep at his sister's, the rectory was clear in case Jeff needed a respite from his house of mourning; understandably, he'd missed choir all week, nor served

THE HOLY HUGS OF FATHER S.

Mass. But Father didn't see him. Out taking a walk, said Carol. But she seemed glad of the company as they sat on the patio sipping G&Ts.

WE ARE CHRIST began filming the next day. Box trucks drew up between church and convent, and cameras, trucks, rails, reflectors, booms, Klieg lights and Fresnel lenses were loaded into the church. Electricians got busy laying cables from the utility room.

But the movie crew's interference with parish operations turned out to be minimal, and of course school was out for Easter week. The director and his crew went off every day to follow their young protagonists. They stalked Johnny Capistrano on his newspaper route as he winged the Washington *Star* at neighbors' carports. Beth G. they filmed playing with her little brother at Wheaton Regional, lifting him up to crawl through an empty engine intake of the F7U Cutlass jetfighter parked near the sandbox. Mark K., who happened to be a Senate page, walked down Capitol corridors greeted by beaming personages who easily descried the camera trundling behind him. Linda Q. chose a wedding gown with her mother as she discussed the big family she hoped to have.

Father Schmidt hated that week. Every day, as if to rub it in, Monsignor asked him to hand-carry various articles from the old rectory to the new. He accepted several dinner invitations — bringing his best table manners — and late every afternoon visited the widow Osborne, sitting on her patio, G&T in hand as sunlight filtered through the trees.

But he never managed to see Jeff. Carol every time said he was out taking a walk. In fact, she confided, she was concerned about his long walks—worried about how he was taking his father's death.

"Is he talking about it?" Father asked.

"Won't say a word."

Well, that was reassuring.

"If you'd like, I can talk to him."

"Thank you, Father, I'll suggest it."

SATURDAY DAWNED, Father's second-to-last full day at St. Jude's, and the day Mass was to be filmed.

Monsignor said he was nervous about only one thing: Would the people come? In olden times, he sighed, the Church might have insured attendance by handing out indulgences—knocking a year off Purgatory, say, in return for spending a day in Hell being a movie extra.

But there was no need for nervousness. Even as Monsignor donned his green silken vestments (matching the new altar cloth) cars were converging on the blacktop and parishioners hurrying inside, greeting one another with, "Hello, *star!*" and eager to place themselves within camera range.

When at last Father Schmidt struck up the choir (lacking Jeff's alto, but everybody understood) in *Holy God, We Praise Thy Name,* the congregation joined in heartily and Monsignor Brannick marched out preceded by his two best-looking altar boys (Conor and Ricky, lookers of Irish stock), gratified to find the church packed as for Midnight Mass.

"*Cut!*" called the director from the side. "Once more, if you please, Monsignor... *Action!*"

"*Cut!*" "*Cut!*" "*Cut!*" "*Print!*" It took five tries to film

— *THE HOLY HUGS OF FATHER S.* —

Monsignor walking out, but the director finally seemed happy.

The Mass was not a valid one. The Host Monsignor eventually raised heavenwards (nine times) remained bread, as did those he distributed at "communion." But that's Hollywood for you.

The day crawled along. The thrill of *being in a movie!* wore off with the grind of every retake. Everything took hours. Camera set-ups were interminable, involving tape measures and light meters and rearranging lights. Unexpectedly, nerves got to Johnny Capistrano singing his solo; several takes were required. The director, sensing restlessness, took to giving little pep talks, and Monsignor reminded his parishioners of what Catholics do when faced with annoyance: *"Offer it up! Offer it up!"*

Father Schmidt meanwhile made sure his choir sounded as good as it possibly could.

Finally an hour's break was called for a late lunch.

Everybody left, but not everyone returned; a new exasperation that meant that, for continuity's sake, the director had to reposition congregants (and later fudge the editing). Filming resumed, the camera cruising up and down the aisles like a cannon as it bore in on Mark K. or Linda Q.

The scene that went most smoothly was the 1:47 homily, the timing specified for the narration that was to play over it. Monsignor nailed it in one take, inviting everybody to the new rectory's open house after filming ended, noting that it would also be a "wrap party," a welcome to his new auxiliary Father Heath and, of course, a farewell reception for beloved Father Schmidt. There would be refreshments, he added.

When at 5:15 the director announced that only the Kiss of Peace remained, everybody did it perfectly the first time, with even an overabundance of enthusiasm.

"*Print!*"

We Are Christ was a wrap.

Everyone headed for the new rectory. It had been an exhausting day, but at least St. Jude's had yet to institute another Vatican II reform—Saturday-evening Mass—so the priests were off the clock for the day.

Father saw someone unfolding himself from a Volkswagen Beetle—the new auxiliary. He was dismayed to find him so big, good-looking and *young*. Father Heath wouldn't report for duty for some weeks, for although a graduate of Catholic University's Theological College, and already a transitional deacon, he had yet to be ordained.

Father Heath—or was it still Mr. Heath?—stood quietly beside the pastor as Monsignor unceasingly thanked parishioners for his splendid new home.

Father Schmidt ascertained that Father Heath wouldn't be working with the choir.

"Alas, I'm no singer. But Monsignor says Mr. Grimes is stepping up?"

The rectory was a mob scene. Parishioners carried plastic glasses of soda pop through the rooms, critically inspecting what their money was buying, though actually pleased at the opulence. Oh, there were last-minute glitches—the garbage disposal wasn't installed yet, a showerhead dripped, one parquet floor needed to be refinished. But it was a stately and spacious house, furnished with Woody's and Hecht's best. A moving van would bring the men's-club furniture over later in the week.

— *THE HOLY HUGS OF FATHER S.* —

The congratulations on his promotion felt like mockery to Father Schmidt. It grated every time somebody said, "Oh, Father, sad for us, but such good news for you!"

Meanwhile the director and crew of *We Are Christ* waxed enthusiastic about what they had in the can; the choir came across *beautifully*.

The open house ended. Father retreated upstairs to what was to have been his study, listening as people left, watching them find their cars and drive away. Then, nibbling leftover potato chips, he wandered the rooms bitterly, an exile.

And all because he tried to comfort a boy whose father died.

The next day, Sunday, the tired priests said their usual rota of Masses—Father three and Monsignor two, including High Mass.

Afterwards, Father Schmidt and his choristers trudged to their room to disrobe. It was time to say goodbye. Eyes moist, men and boys presented little parting gifts, saying, "We'll miss you, Father, but we're so happy for you: a parish of your own!"

As the boys filed out, Father, sobbing, kissed each full on the lips.

Before going off to his sister's, Monsignor insisted on taking Father to early dinner at the Olney Inn, where he expressed gratitude for his help over the years, particularly with the choir.

Father thanked him, too; it was the gracious thing to do, howevermuch he seethed inside.

Later, locking up the new rectory after bringing over the last of Monsignor's mother's china, Father realized that he could stay the night if he wanted; there was no one to say him nay.

Dashing home to pick up his suitcase and some bedding, he settled into his suite with a deeply unhappy sigh.

11.

At 7:00 a.m. on an April morning dripping with rain Father Schmidt said his final Mass at St. Jude's. He raced through it, but added three minutes to its length by addressing a homily of gratitude to his dozen regulars for being there day after day, year after year. He told them he'd miss them, with some satisfaction adding that until Father Heath's installation Monsignor would take early Mass himself.

As he stepped back from the lectern, several called out, "We'll miss you, too, Father! But congratulations!"

After hanging up his vestments, he thanked his altar boy, by prior arrangement left his keys in the poor box and walked out to his car, already loaded with his suitcase and boxes. Exchanging a wave with a nun too far away to identify, he drove away from St. Jude's.

His first stop was the Hot Shoppe for breakfast. It was a cheerful scene, until a parishioner waylaid him and slathered him with congratulations.

It was a relief to get back into the Fury.

His route lay south through novel parts of Montgomery County, then Prince George's County, Charles County,

Anne Arundel County, Calvert County into St. Mary's County—rural terra incognita. The roads, narrow and empty, wound past tobacco fields and barns almost open-air in construction. One hamlet of wooden shanties had a store whose window still bore a NO COLORED sign. Father wondered if it were a collector's item.

The radio began to give out as the countryside became wooded. He turned it off when he could raise nothing but a distant Christian station, driving on under a canopy of trees that veiled the misty road behind him.

It was like driving back in time. Didn't John Wilkes Booth roam this countryside for weeks after shooting Lincoln? Nothing had changed. The landscape was still that of Civil War times, a slower era with a doomed feel to it. He passed a courthouse where a lone soldier made of lead stood sentry; he looked Confederate. Confederate flags flew from some of the houses. There were few road signs; Father divined that they'd be superfluous: You had to know the region, seeing as you were driving in it.

Clearly it was poor, too. Houses were rundown, with collapsed porches and out buildings. The few other cars on the road got older and older, soon were mostly turtle-shaped sedans from the '40s and '30s in lusterless browns and grays, cars you just didn't see around Washington anymore. Then, by golly, a Model A Ford came tooling along! The few people he saw watched the Fury pass like a rocketship.

Civil War? No, *earlier*—back to the *Ark* and the *Dove* and the founders of the Catholic Church in America.

Approaching Bullnose—surely an odd name for a maritime community?—the trees thinned to the right side of the road and Father saw the broad estuary of the

—THE HOLY HUGS OF FATHER S.—

Potomac merging with Chesapeake Bay beneath an amplified sky. Beside many of the houses—some on stilts—were boats tied up at docks or drawn up on trailers, with nets spread. Some houses' mail boxes sat atop old naval mines. Amidst signs proclaiming fish and shellfish for sale were stacks of crab traps and the hooks and winders of the mussel trade.

Welcome to Bullnose Founded 1659 Pop. 242, said the rotting sign. Father Schmidt saw a gas station, wooden storefronts, a brick post office and, next to it, St. Datian's poky old frame church and rectory, both painted in shades of green resembling mold.

Parking on gravel between them, Father got out stiffly and stretched, and discovered that his new back yard was in fact an ancient graveyard. He could see no living soul. Walking to the rectory's front door, he found it locked, and stood flummoxed before deciding to look around the church. At least the rain had stopped.

The church was unlocked. The interior was musty and dark. Letting his eyes adjust, Father saw that the walls were the color of dust, the windows the cheapest stained-glass. Over the altar—still facing the back wall—was a not very delectable Christ. Was that birdshit caking Him? Floorboards creaking, Father walked into the sacristy and found cupboards full of tatty vestments reeking of mothballs, along with a walled-off toilet with a cigarette butt afloat in it. Heaving a sigh, he went back outdoors.

An old man across the way slammed shut his door and walked towards him.

"Leif welcome you to St. Datian's," he said.

"Sorry?" said Father.

The man handed him a door key, spat and receded.

Father unlocked the rectory and went through the rooms of his new home, his heart sinking at how stuffy and old-fashioned they were, decorated to ecclesiastical fashions of approximately 1900. The walls were a soiled tan or dirty salmon, the floors dun and scuffed. Frayed curtains hung across yellowed window shades.

Father brought his things inside and in the bedroom down the hall stood regarding the caved-in, sheetless mattress. At least it was a double bed. All volition vanished, he curled up on top of it.

It had come to this.

He didn't know how long he lay there, nigglingly aware that he'd have to rouse himself at some point if he wished to eat, or sleep in a made bed, or find out if the phone worked, before there came a knock at the front door.

Moaning, Father Schmidt rolled over to wait it out.

But the knock came again, and again.

Father came groaning to his feet and went down the hallway, seeing a figure through the front door's little window.

He opened the door. The man standing there in clerical collar and black jacket looked at Father with a smile of complicity, amusement in his eyes. Not half bad looking, if rather glossy, he was only just younger than Father Schmidt.

"Yes?" said Father.

"Father Schmidt?" asked the visitor, extending his hand. "I'm Father Robin, from St. Martin's—next parish over? I've been working St. Datian's since Father Stefan died. Can't imagine how glad I am you're here!"

Father shook his hand and brought him indoors. Asking permission, Father Robin retrieved the bourbon he'd left in the pantry, and soon was toasting Father Schmidt in the parlor.

"Welcome to a most special place," he said, adding, as if with quotation marks around it, *"St. Mary's County."*

Father Schmidt said, "Driving down felt like going back a century in time."

"Only one? Try two, even *three*. It's old, it's slow and nothing ever happens—but that's its charm, too, I think you'll find. We're away from the madding crowd. Life goes on without the outside world."

"You—*like* it?"

"Cards on the table?" said Father Robin. "I was up in the District, auxiliary at Peter-and-Paul's? The coming man, too, you might say, when, regrettably, two years ago, I blotted my copybook.

"The Archbishop hauled me in, placed me over the trapdoor in front of his desk, reamed me out and pulled the lever. Woke up in St. Mary's County.

"Oh, they built it up: 'Your own parish, Father, think of that!' and 'The *Ark* and the *Dove*, Father, think of that!'"

Father Schmidt smiled bleakly.

"So I'll never be the Bishop of Rome or any place else. I've reached my peak in Holy Mother Church. But that's not the worst thing in the world either, Father. I'm finding compensations. You might even say I'm comfortable here."

"Well, good."

"Hope it's not speaking out of turn to guess that maybe you blotted your copybook, too? So it's off to St. Mary's County with you! But we're not alone here, and like exiles everywhere we make our own way, even manage to have some fun from time to time. Friendly group, you'll find us, of—how to put it?—*like-minded* guys. You'll fit right in."

"More?" Father Schmidt asked, holding out the bottle. "When you knocked I was about to read Vespers."

"Let's do it," said Father Robin and, drinks refreshed, they raced each other through the psalms and prayers of Father Schmidt's breviary. Like old times; he and Monsignor sometimes used to read their Offices over cocktails.

Then Father Robin drove Father Schmidt down the road in his scarlet MG-TC to a waterfront restaurant, the family who ran it flustered and honored to have *two* priests as guests. Slot machines rattling at the wall, their teenaged son carried out plates with his tongue poking out one side of his mouth, serious and intent, and Father Robin kicked Father Schmidt under the table.

And told him, "Say what you will about Southern Maryland, the seafood's terrific: the *crabs? oysters? scallops? clams? shrimp?*"

That night, finally finding the sheets and making his bed, Father fell asleep feeling less alone, even if Father Robin had declined his invitation to stay the night.

12.

FOR THE REMAINDER of his home stay after the funeral, Ron drove the Mustang into the District every morning. He unpinned the Herblock cartoons from Dent's cubicle and cleaned out his desk, finding stray mementos—a medallion from a White House Correspondents dinner, a PT-109 tie clasp, snapshots of Dent with JFK at Hyannis Port.

Dent's colleagues took him to lunch at Paul Young's downstairs, exactly Ron's idea of a glamorous restaurant, and asked whether he aspired to journalism. No; but he did accompany one on a round of Capitol interviews.

For six featureless weeks—until school ended—Carol picked Jeff up every day and drove out to the cemetery. It was a schlep, but better to be doing *something*. There Jeff observed minute changes to their particular mound of clay on the plain of headstones. Sifted by wind and rain, it eroded, and the flowers laid against it withered and vanished as the plot awaited its stone. Carol did her weeping behind closed doors, and Jeff—adding to the list of things he felt guilty about—had no more tears.

He stopped serving as an altar boy, and when the dance lessons moved elsewhere—so as not to impose, Mrs. Adams said—stopped going to them, too. The boy who in class always raised his arm, ready with either the correct answer or an interesting one, now sat quiet and distracted. He could even get snippy with the nuns, but they were tolerant, and he'd stored up six years of goodwill. He found his friends suddenly different as, chary of him for having lost his Dad, they concentrated on their glide paths to graduation. People said he was taking his father's death hard.

He returned to choir, however, under Mr. Grimes's direction continued to enjoy feeling on his fingertips the power of their voices. The closest he came to talking about anything was passing on to his brother Conor's tale of Father's farewell kisses. Ron raised his eyebrows, but said nothing.

Jeff found solace in two directions.

In reading, first of all. He plundered his father's bookshelves, which held (as he liked to boast) some 3,000 volumes. Books carried him into new dimensions, absorbed him for hours at a time. He read *The House of the Seven Gables, David Copperfield,* James T. Farrell's *Studs Lonigan* and John Dos Passos' *U.S.A.* trilogies, and *Brideshead Revisited* (he loved it!). So long as he was reading, so long as he lived inside his own head, life was bearable.

His other solace was the opposite—getting outdoors and out of himself. He took to walking the miles-long path bordering the stream that flowed past the foot of Trent Lane. Northwest Branch is a tributary of the Anacostia River, which wends its way through Washington before emptying into the Potomac. It was only 20 feet across and a foot deep, the water flowing brown beneath scummy suds, but the woods lining it were alive with birds, squirrels, rabbits, raccoons, groundhogs, possums, with rumor of fox and bobcat. Honeysuckle grew riotously, along with sumac and poison ivy. Closer to the ground were May apples, even lady's slipper. And the birds! Cacophonous, especially towards sunset.

Walking miles without meeting anyone, Jeff felt newly alive to the scene, felt a new correspondence between the woods' blossoming fecundity and his own body; closer to being healed every time he went outdoors, as though life didn't take place solely inside his own head after all, but shared in Nature.

As the house emptied of reminders of Dent's death—the covered dishes' contents eaten or tossed out, dishes washed and returned with effusive thanks, cards and letters filed away—Carol spoke vaguely of needing to make plans. "I might sell the Lincoln," she said one day.

No decision about Jeff's schooling needed to be made, though. Having been admitted to Prep, he would attend as a day student at least through freshman year. After that, they'd see.

Fortunately the pressures weren't financial. Not only did Dent leave a good stock portfolio, but Orbs, Inc. would continue their Blue Cross indefinitely, even help with school fees, and there was a hefty life insurance policy. Carol would be awash in cash for quite some time to come.

When Jeff went out for his walk, she would remind him, "Dinner at 6:00" from her favorite Danish modern chair, smoking, glass at her elbow, feet on the footstool, immersed in *Seven Days in May* or *The Ugly American*.

After dinner was done she transferred—bundled up, if need be—to the patio to continue drinking and smoking while the sun sank behind the trees.

One evening—*Paperback Writer* on his turntable—Jeff looked up *rape* in the dictionary and pondered the definitions of noun and verb as *forced sexual intercourse*.

But didn't the very word *intercourse* imply an exchange? And doesn't exchange imply the opposite of forced?

Had he been forced? Not at first, certainly. His body betrayed him, betrayed its interest, joining in until, too late, it proved too weak to fight off Father's frenzy. Had he cooperated to the extent that *rape* didn't apply?

So was he *not* a victim, after all?

He didn't want to be, and if the whole thing was his fault—he wasn't.

13.

FATHER SCHMIDT INVITED St. Jude's choir down to Bullnose for a Memorial Day barbecue. He meant it to help make up for the JFK birthday Mass invitation being rescinded, which he knew had to be painful for his boys.

They were happy about the excursion. School was done—all but the 8th grade's graduation the following Saturday—and Mr. Grimes knew they'd like to see Father Schmidt again. At first he thought of arranging a convoy of cars, but wound up chartering a school bus and driver instead. That would let the men drink beer with their barbecue.

Everybody showed up at St. Jude's in time to get on board. Naturally what the choir was singing as the bus pulled away—making their parents smile—was *Ninety-Nine Bottles of Beer*.

The singing petered out while they were still passing new housing developments. Soon they were in unfamiliar countryside with an ancient air: tobacco fields, manor houses, shacks. The men at the front of the bus ignored the boisterousness behind them. They had kids of their own.

Jeff sat in the back with his friends. He felt he had no choice but to attend the barbecue. If he stayed away people would wonder why, maybe hit on the reason he wished to avoid Father. So he sat joshing with the others as Conor started slapping everyone's thighs to see if they jiggled, and had Jeff slap his.

It was a long drive down to St. Mary's County. Passing under fresh veils of forest canopy, they went through smaller and smaller towns and villages, until nothing contradicted the notion they'd gone back in time but the sight of telephone poles or the occasional car, invariably ancient.

Finally the bus reached Bullnose and, picking its way past wooden storefronts, pulled up at an unprosperous-looking grouping: St. Datian's. The tombstones behind it were slanted slabs of mossy stone backed by dark, dark woods.

"We're here, boys!" called Mr. Grimes. "Remember, our hymn first."

Pushing and shoving, the choirboys got off the bus as Father Schmidt appeared in his usual black, along with another man, in shorts and polo shirt, whom he introduced as Father Robin; Father Robin was already taking advantage of Vatican II's relaxed clergy dress code. In their motley of jeans, shorts and T-shirts the boys took their places, Mr. Grimes blew his pitch pipe and they sang *O What Could My Jesus Do More* in Father Schmidt's acapella arrangement.

Father's eyes filled, and Father Robin patted his shoulder. It was so lovely a couple wearing aprons came from behind the rectory to listen.

"*Beautiful,*" said Father Schmidt. "Thank you!

— *THE HOLY HUGS OF FATHER S.* —

Mr. Grimes, you should be proud!"

"Beautiful!" echoed Father Robin.

"OK, everybody," Father said, "we'll eat lunch in a minute. Mr. and Mrs. Clapperson are giving us hamburgers and hot dogs, and later, for dinner, their famous barbecued chicken. Hope you brought your appetites! Now go find the soda pop and potato chips."

The boys dispersed. They found the chips and, in coolers steaming with dry ice, bottles of Teem, RC Cola and Dr Pepper. St. Datian's graveyard and lawns, including the one laid out as a baseball field, were freshly mowed, and to do the cooking Father Schmidt had engaged a parish couple whose chicken was the rage of Southern Maryland, which they traversed every weekend pulling a yellow trailer behind their station wagon.

The boys scarfed down their burgers and franks. Afterwards most took bats, balls and gloves to the field next door, chose up sides — a few of the men joined in, to fill out the numbers — and began a game, everybody swatting gnats from their eyes. The gnats were even worse here than at home, and it was even hotter and muggier.

Jeff and Conor walked over to inspect the church.

"*Sheesh*," remarked Conor. "Cradle of the American Church? Believe it."

"Parish of his own? *Wow*."

They went down ramshackle Bullnose Street and back without comment, feeling something like space aliens, before Conor sighed, "Let's play ball."

He being the best pitcher, his appearance was cheered. Jeff was relegated to the outfield. The bus driver umpired, while the men looked on benignly, sitting on lawn chairs, beers in hand, near the priests.

The game unfolded as baseball does, leisurely, save at moments of intense action, boys with loose-jointed athleticism stretching, running, hurling themselves into dirt, leaping, batting, throwing. In its slow progress and intermittent excitements, it seemed of a piece with older times.

The priests watched closely, putting their heads together to confer.

Of one batter Father Schmidt murmured, "What would you say, five?"

"I *like* skinny," answered Father Robin. "Strong *seven!*"

Of another boy he said, "Today I'd say *four,* but watch out next year."

"And the pitcher?"

"Oh, the pitcher! *Nine,* but if you said *ten* I wouldn't put up much of a fight."

They giggled.

"Oh, yes, let's see if he'll play for *our* team."

"Think he's a switch hitter?"

"Like to find out."

Mr. Grimes asked Father Schmidt if he'd formed a new choir.

"On hold for now," he answered. "It's a small parish."

"And how's your Fury treating you?"

"I love it, Mr. Grimes."

When Jeff came up to bat, Father Schmidt elbowed Father Robin.

"Here he is."

"Gawky. But sweet. Seven? Eight?"

When Father Schmidt told his friend about his night with Jeff, Father Robin probed just a little. "Was he *hard...?* OK, and did he *come...?* He *liked* it, Father—end of story."

— *THE HOLY HUGS OF FATHER S.* —

The priests were prevailed upon to join the game. Father Schmidt struck out, but Father Robin homered.

Meanwhile, the Clappersons prepared their chicken, placing marinated carcasses in flat wire frames, spraying them with more marinade, placing the frames over charcoal. The broiled chicken smelled wonderful, and would prove to be excellent eating.

When Mr. Grimes realized that part of the infield had found the beer, he brought the game to a close—Jeff's side won—and they got ready to eat dinner.

Lining up, the boys were served paper plates laden with chicken, corn on the cob, baked beans, coleslaw, potato salad and corn bread, and told there was plenty more. For half an hour things were quiet under the old trees as the sun started to go down. After an interval, cake and ice cream with syrups and nuts were served up. Boys and men murmured comfortably, spooning ice cream. No one wished to voice the obvious fact that it was time to think about going home.

Mr. and Mrs. Clapperson cleaned up and drove off, everyone calling their thanks.

In the gloaming, fireflies began to spark, blinking their warm, lingering yellow. Some of the younger boys, catching at them, rubbed their luminescence over their pants. Coming up behind Johnny, Conor touched his shoulder, yelled, "You're *it!*" and skittered away. Instantly it was a riot of boys running around the baseball field and graveyard tagging one another amidst cries of panic or triumph. The men looked on benignly, but stayed out of the way, nor did the dead protest the overhead tramp of boys pivoting and sprinting.

"You're *it!*" yelled a boy tagging Jeff, and Jeff, a fast

runner, charged after the next nearest one—and vanished.

Everybody blinked. What happened? It was inexplicable.

Then they heard him screaming.

Jeff screamed, but it was muffled and distant. Perplexed, everybody hustled over to where he was last seen and ringed the open grave he'd fallen into—freshly dug for Mr. Grady, full seven feet deep and wet at the bottom—until Father Schmidt broke through, prostrated himself at the edge and reached into the void.

"Jeff, take my hands," he urged, feeling blindly. "Guys, hold my legs."

Jeff grabbed Father's hands with both his and was pulled out, shaken up—*very* shaken up—but at least not buried alive.

Father smothered him in a hug, nuzzling his hair despite his muddy front and face, and Jeff broke away shrieking until calmed by his friends. Though almost right away everybody else found it funny—*to fall into an open grave!*—the humor of it escaped him.

It was time to go home, anyway. The bus driver started the engine and, Mr. Grimes blowing his pitch pipe, the choir burst into another of Father's inspired arrangements. Touched, he signed his blessing over them and encouraged everybody to grab the last sodas for the ride.

The bus drove off. Father Schmidt heaved a mighty sigh, but Father Robin clapped him on the shoulder and handed him a Schlitz.

That night Jeff had a nightmare that recurred for years: Father Schmidt embracing him in an open grave.

He quit choir the following week.

14.

ST. JUDE'S FIRST graduation took place in the church, proud families looking on as 26 girls came singing down the left side of the aisle, 24 boys down the right. Forming such processions had been second nature to them for six years. For the last time wearing school uniforms, they marched symmetrically and passed in front of the old altar to receive their diplomas from Monsignor Brannick, whose speech informed them that graduation is not an end but a beginning.

After the soda-pop reception in the cafeteria, Carol took Jeff to the Hot Shoppe, where they exchanged congratulations with other graduates.

The next day Jeff took over mowing a neighbor's lawn.

And he met Gerald, a Storybook Forest resident who'd just finished 8th grade at Garrett Prep and was entering 9th grade there—Jeff's class—in the fall. His mother, Ruth, promoted their friendship by taking them to Baskin-Robbins for ice cream cones. She also hit it off with Carol, who was to share car-pool duties, getting their sons (plus another nearby freshman, Vance, whose mother was exempt from car pool because she had ten children) to Georgia Avenue to meet Prep's bus morning and evening. This was the first year the bus would venture so deep into suburbia on a route that started in Northwest.

Gerald was already working a summer job for a fresh Prep graduate, David, who was headed to Harvard in the fall: painting houses. It was practically a professional affair, save that—to evade Maryland's work-permit laws—customers were limited to David's relatives and parents' friends. Delighted to be asked to join the crew, Jeff moved his lawn mowing to weekends, despite customer gripes about the noise impinging on days of leisure.

Every morning David picked them up in his VW microbus with ladders on the roof and drove them to whatever house in Silver Spring, Kensington or Rockville they were painting, where they would set up and work all day.

Scraping was the hard part. They scraped loose and blistered paint off weathered siding, occasionally from brick; *scraped scraped scraped*, telling each other as they sweated—paint flecking the sweat—that at least they were getting in shape. Then they slapped down fresh paint.

At lunchtime they piled into the microbus and, sweating shirtless shoulder to shoulder, went off to Burger Chef or Kentucky Fried Chicken, then found a shady patch of grass somewhere to eat and fart. David liked to lie back on his elbows and raise one extended leg to toot as familiarly as a fireman.

It was hard, honest work that they did conscientiously—paid in cash, too.

Gerald was a nice boy, dark and good-looking, but shared none of Jeff's interests, and made him nervous

— *THE HOLY HUGS OF FATHER S.* —

when he proposed sleeping out in a tent in his backyard. Though this chimed in eerily with his old fantasy, Jeff put him off from week to week. His fantasies were gone. He kept his hands to himself, just didn't want to do it anymore. He thought, *"If I hadn't gone with him, if I'd refused to watch TV or drink a beer."*

Several times that summer he awoke to the tickling sensations of a wet dream.

He stopped believing in God, too. He realized it abruptly the day a neighbor pulled over near where he was mowing to talk to her kids, then drove on, not realizing the kids' cocker spaniel had wandered beneath the car. What kind of God but one promoting random pain would allow that?

Jeff gave the Roman Catholic Church full credit for expanding his imagination, much like the *Superman* comic books he'd loved as a kid. But that was about it.

Even so, as he pushed the Toro, he was wagering his immortal soul: "If I don't reach that hedge before the tenth *ever*, I'll be in Hell *forever* and *ever* and *ever* and *ever* and *ever* and *ever* and *ever* and *ever* and *ever*—"

Every day after dinner he took a walk in the lingering light, then a bath—reading *Pride and Prejudice, A Farewell to Arms, The Adventures of Augie March*—before going to bed and reading there, feeling at a grateful remove as the air-conditioning vents softly hissed.

Then he dreamed of *scraping, scraping, scraping* or of being embraced by Father Schmidt in an open grave.

15.

SUMMER IN ST. MARY'S County was unbelievably steamy. The humidity was absolute, the sun scorching. Father Schmidt left off wearing black, but never looked the epitome of cool, as Father Robin did, hooking his sunglasses in the V of his polo shirt as he climbed out of the MG in Bermuda shorts.

One day Father Robin invited Father Schmidt over to St. Martin's.

"It's the Teen Club car wash," he said. "Our hot weather moneymaker? Keeps the kids cool, too. They'll wash your Fury like nobody's business for two bucks, wax it for another two."

"All right," said Father.

That Saturday he was astonished to find St. Martin's parking lot thronged with teenagers waving *Car Wash* signs at passing drivers as balloons bobbed. All the boys were shirtless. Father pulled the Fury to the end of the line, which wound its way to where a battery of drenched, half-naked boys worked with hoses, chamois, sponges and buckets of sudsy water.

—THE HOLY HUGS OF FATHER S.—

When his turn came Father made sure his windows were shut tight and sat back to enjoy the show. Through soapy glass he enjoyed delectable gardens of young male flesh, studied the action of chests, arms, underarms and faces as, with serious mien, boys labored over his fenders. Taut bellies pressing against his windows, every prospect pleased.

A lad slapped his roof—*done*—and Father proffered $2 through the top of his window, plus a $2 tip, and moved up for waxing. More young men—shirtless, if not so wet—swarmed over the Fury. The play of their muscles mesmerized Father, biceps swelling as they rubbed in one direction, triceps stiffening as they buffed in the other. Some of the boys he recognized as his own parishioners.

He enjoyed their interplay, too, chafing one another and catcalling the girls waiting behind with fresh cloths. Invisible to them despite his clerical collar—or because of it—Father reveled in the persiflage flying amidst bare flesh.

He proffered another $2, and another tip.

Father Robin strolled up and Father Schmidt lowered his window. Now he looked embarrassed.

"Some of these kids are *my* parishioners—"

"Ah, but you don't have a school," Father Robin reminded him. "Your kids attend ours, so naturally they join our Teen Club. You should get involved. We do all kinds of fun things: Dances, cookouts, litter pick-ups. Overnights."

"*Overnights?*"

"Camping out? *Great* fun."

Father Schmidt looked alert. Before going home, he pledged to help with Father Robin's Teen Club, and had also conceived the dream of founding St. Datian's School.

16.

CAROL RENTED A COTTAGE for the last two weeks of August. She and Dent discovered North Carolina's Outer Banks after he came off the 1960 campaign trail, and had returned every summer since. This year she rented their favorite cottage on the beach a few miles above Kitty Hawk's pier — a stucco one-story with a separate wing for the boys — and invited her two closest Denver cousins.

Bunny and Hortense (the only Hortense Jeff ever knew) arrived a few days before the rental started and enjoyed being tourists in the meantime, though Carol assured them that in the middle of August no one was around and nothing open. But they wanted to see the National Gallery of Art, so — his summer job concluded, and finding a substitute to mow his neighbor's lawn — Jeff accompanied them. Hortense driving the Mustang as if it suited her, he directed her to the cavernous Capital Garage on New York Avenue, a setting suggestive of spy rendezvous.

Soon they were in cool galleries surrounded by famous paintings. Bunny and Hortense oohed at those they recognized, according each a respectful inspection. Jeff

— *THE HOLY HUGS OF FATHER S.* —

came to love the National Gallery on school field trips, until St. Jude's was banned on account of an unfortunate incident: While their guide explained how Manet had slashed one big canvas into three separate masterpieces, there was a commotion across the room. When she prevailed on the son of a papal knight to step aside from a Cezanne, everybody saw the spitball on its surface.

Today Jeff was glad to find the Cezanne back on display.

They ate lunch in the cafeteria of tiled walls and stainless steel fixtures.

"*Prep* school!" cried Hortense.

"No *girls?*" Bunny put in.

"No."

"Do you have a girlfriend, Jeff?"

"No."

"Getting interested, though, right?"

"I don't know."

"Fewer distractions, anyway, right?"

"I guess."

"Do you think your mom will move back to Denver now?"

First he'd heard of it. "She's always said she didn't want to live there. She loves her aunts, but—"

"But with your father gone...?" Eyes bright, they regarded him.

"I guess. Maybe."

"If you insist on a Jesuit school, we have Regis. We know it well—*we* three went to St. Mary's."

Their devotion to the Church amazed him. Hortense was divorced and thus barred from receiving the Church's sacraments. Bunny, married for two decades, had told Jeff,

"We've been unhappy for years," but there was no prospect of divorce because that would bar *her* from receiving the sacraments.

After lunch they pushed on. Jeff knew every tourist attraction in the District of Columbia—every single one of them!—but didn't suggest his favorite, the Army Medical Museum, a Victorian repository of gruesome Lincoln assassination memorabilia and pickled fetuses. Instead they entered the Smithsonian's newest branch, the Museum of History and Technology, and spent hours happily tramping past locomotives and First Ladies' inaugural gowns.

They went home exhausted.

THAT SATURDAY THEY convoyed to the beach in both cars. Ron—home for a month before returning to college—tried in the Lincoln to keep up with Hortense in the Mustang. As sections of I-95 were completed every year the route became shorter, but it was still a five-hour slog, culminating in passing the Great Dismal Swamp—whose black waters sprouted dead white trees—and vast peanut fields. As always, Carol stopped at Anna Gallup's fruit stand to buy bushels of tomatoes, figs, peaches, apples, peanuts, watermelon, honeydews and corn. Then, crossing the shaky wooden bridge across Pamlico Sound, and picking up keys and linens at the rental office, they pulled up to their cottage.

Carol and her sons instantly relaxed in the blazing sun and salt breeze, savoring the remoteness, the freedom from TV, radio and telephone.

"No TV?" ventured Hortense.

—THE HOLY HUGS OF FATHER S.—

"Where's the action, Carol?" Bunny asked.

"No action at all," she said. "That's why we love it so."

But Bunny and Hortense too changed into bathing suits, spread their towels and applied their lotions while the boys charged into the breakers.

The wide horizon showed nothing but ocean. Freed by its infinite expanse, happy for the first time all summer, Carol sat on the sand breathing deep while breakers crashed and terns and gulls called.

Eventually Bunny pointed out a ship rounding Cape Hatteras to the south.

Much later a school of flying fish passed, darting silver over the surf.

They weren't quite alone. In both directions families frolicked some thirty yards apart, and an older couple in floppy hats was patiently fishing. Two women passed, eyes to the sand, searching for sea shells.

Meanwhile Ron and Jeff body-surfed, flinging themselves atop breakers, to be carried *(whoosh!)* to the utmost stretch of froth, eye to eye with bubbles percolating up through the sand and sand crabs emerging behind the bubbles.

"That looks like fun," Bunny said.

"Carol, honey," said Hortense, "it's like the ends of the earth here."

"Isn't it just?"

Bunny and Hortense eventually waded into ankle-deep water, surprised at the force of its suction.

That evening they uncorked the first of many bottles of white wine.

Next day, they attended Mass at Holy Redeemer in Kill Devil Hills, a little church hot as "the box" in a prisoner-of-war movie. Congregants started leaking out early.

After his summer of scraping and painting and mowing, Jeff found the sea bracing, its endless cycle of waves curling atop waves cleansing. That first week he read *Kim*, *The Great Gatsby* and *Gulliver's Travels*.

Carol took her cousins grocery shopping at Anderson's, one of the two small grocery stores. Near by the cousins spotted the area's sole restaurant, at a new motel near the pier, and proposed treating everybody for dinner.

Dolling themselves up, they found themselves eating fried fish amongst family groups as they suggested that Carol move back to Denver.

Although she expressed fondness for the city and for her late mother's house on Krameria Street, Carol declared that her life now lay in Washington, or at least in its suburbs, at least for the moment.

Time wore on. It was just to Jeff's taste and his brother's and mother's—sanctified, too, by being their annual routine. As sometimes happened, a sand bar formed across the breakers, so the boys were splashing in unexpectedly shallow waters the day porpoises cavorted near by.

Though Bunny and Hortense made daily forays to the beach, lying slathered and unmoving, growing darker, they also took on a defeated look. But by night with the assistance of wine they came alive, though marveling how "sand just gets *everywhere*."

On Friday they returned from Wink's Grocery and told Carol they'd used the pay phone to call Bunny's husband, and were sorry but had to get home right away. They'd changed their flight reservations. What contingency drew them back early to Denver wasn't clear—*not* an emergency, they insisted—and they were so sorry.

—*THE HOLY HUGS OF FATHER S.*—

Ron ran them up to Norfolk Municipal Airport.

The next week Jeff read *Jane Eyre, Life on the Mississippi* and *Catch-22*.

They convoyed home Saturday of Labor Day weekend.

17.

THE CATHOLIC STANDARD, the Archdiocese's weekly newspaper, announced that the world premiere of *We Are Christ* would take place at St. Jude's September 6, the day after Labor Day, a month ahead of its TV broadcast. Archbishop O'Boyle himself hoped to attend.

Father Schmidt saw the notice and yearned to be there. At first he half-expected Monsignor to telephone an invitation—possibly including an overnight stay—in recognition of his contribution to the film.

But none came.

Which made him miserable.

SEPTEMBER 6 arrived. The paper said the showing was scheduled for 7:00 o'clock. Father Schmidt told himself that if he set off for St. Jude's as if for a long drive in the country, he could change his mind and loop back home at any point, no one the wiser, or continue onwards, just as he pleased.

After the showing—*if* he attended—he'd have to drive home in the dark or take a motel room, or maybe

Monsignor would do the hospitable thing, after all?

Telling his housekeeper he'd be eating out, Father got in the Fury.

He took it sedately up Bullnose Street, a tableau as still as an Edward Hopper painting whose every brick, every plank he loathed. At the flashing yellow stoplight that was the hamlet's boast he pulled into the Esso station and had the attendant fill 'er up.

Then Father pulled out and began to zoom under the veils of leafy boughs overhead, now imperceptibly beginning to thin. It was like opening door after door. Every hamlet passed, every curve taken opened another door. The countryside opened up with tobacco fields and cornfields. Abruptly the radio returned, blasting *Sunshine Superman*. Maintaining his priestly expression, Father gunned the engine to pass the old sedans loitering behind a tractor.

He felt like a bankrobber on the way, if not to rob, at least to *case* a bank. He didn't imagine that Monsignor would welcome him. Instead, thunderclouds would boil on his brow, he might in an uninviting tone ask what he wanted. But surely the parishioners would be glad to see their old auxiliary again? If Father Schmidt dared, just *dared*, he could pull it off.

Well, he'd dared worse.

In fact, Father's guilt about Jeff Osborne was easing into what amounted almost to pride—a certain admiration of himself for having the nerve to do what he did, for being such a *smooth operator*.

His new friend was helping him become looser, more self-accepting.

"You're so inhibited!" Father Robin would crow.

"Loosen up already! Isn't that life's big lesson? *Loosen up.*"

Father felt less confident, though, approaching St. Jude's and seeing the blacktop filling up with cars. He almost turned around. After all, *The Catholic Standard* also said the Archdiocese's Sunday morning TV showcase would broadcast *We Are Christ* in October.

Of course, to pick up a TV signal Father would have to journey to civilization somewhere, just as he was doing now.

Then he realized that he could (after a fashion) attend the premiere without having to show himself or speak to anybody. He knew the layout of St. Jude's like the back of his hand. The 16 mm. projector would be aimed at the screen pulled down the cafeteria's east wall. Father could park alongside the convent, walk over to the cafeteria's south wall and, hanging back near the corner where the kitchen joined the church, see everything through the windows—hear everything, too, the windows doubtless being louvered open in the warm evening.

The church would be empty, the driveway unused, the nuns all in the cafeteria trying to give each other better seats: No one would see him.

And though it was unlikely anybody would exit through the door in that south wall, if perchance somebody *did,* at the very worst it would be, "Oh, Father Schmidt, what are you doing out *here?* Do come in!"

So Father parked the Fury in the convent driveway, made the exposed, heart-pounding walk to the shadowed kitchen corner and crept up to the cafeteria windows. Already it was twilight; the sun would set before the film ended.

Craning from the shadows, he peered into the lighted

—THE HOLY HUGS OF FATHER S.—

room. Excited parishioners were filling rows of folding chairs, greeting one another with "Hello, *star!*" The Archbishop apparently was a no-show, but Father saw Monsignor Brannick standing with Father Heath, spiffy in his new clerical collar. Monsignor happening to glance at the windows, Father took two steps back, but already it was too dark for him to be seen.

He heard someone ask whether Father Schmidt was coming.

Monsignor looked at his auxiliary. "We didn't hear from Father Schmidt, did we?"

"No, Monsignor," answered Father Heath.

Their tone told him to stay where he was.

That tone—coupled with the Archbishop's absence—told him more, in fact. That St. Jude's had been chosen for the movie was a huge compliment to Monsignor Brannick, but losing his longtime auxiliary as a child molester? He'd never make bishop now. In fact, only days after Father Schmidt's posting to St. Datian's, Archbishop O'Boyle filled Bishop Hannon's empty chair with Monsignor Herrman.

It hadn't before struck Father that, in breaching the confessional, Monsignor had knowingly thrown away his prospects of a bishop's hat; had he stayed mum, he might well have been elevated himself. Father had to respect that.

Well, he always respected Monsignor, just never much liked him.

Unbelievably, Father then heard Monsignor telling his favorite story, a chestnut everybody in the parish (save for Father Heath) had heard a hundred times, about his immigrant grandfather's early failure in the New World: After slaving for years as a bartender near Yankee Stadium, he'd saved up enough money to rent a bar himself and renovate it into the tavern of his dreams. For the transformation he hired a contractor he knew from church, no less trustworthy a gent than the usher of the children's Mass.

When the contractor took all his money but did no work, Monsignor's grandfather remonstrated with his pastor, who was dismayed: "Oh, but Mr. Brannick, we let him usher the children's Mass because *there* he can only steal pennies!"

Father Heath dutifully laughed.

Monsignor added that it shows how the Church likes to handle things.

Soon the lights went off and the projector, operated by tech-savvy Sister Briana, began to roll.

We Are Christ turned out to be a professional production, if heavy on liturgy. Footage of young parishioners' daily rounds—Father loved seeing Johnny Capistrano pitching his newspapers with an arm like Sandy Koufax's—was spliced into scenes of Monsignor saying the updated Mass. As the narrator jauntily described the changes Vatican II brought to the liturgy, the camera traveled its rails, panning across choirboys' faces. And, oh, but they sounded *heavenly!*

The lights flicked on as the credits began to roll, and with surprise Father noticed the entire tanned Osborne family—Carol, Ron and Jeff—sitting in the last row near the windows, Jeff at the end practically within reach. *Jeff!*

Father's instantaneous erection energized him. He could go inside, greet Carol, shake Ron's hand and hug Jeff, sweep him off to the Hot Shoppe to discuss the film and see how his vocation was coming along, afterwards maybe go to a motel.

But as people got up (expressions glazed with disappointment: *Do I really look like that?*), Father judged it the better part of valor to slip away. Hastening to the Fury, he drove off, foot heavy on the gas, brights on as he sped south into the heart of darkness, door after door closing— *slamming*—behind him, sealing in his backwards travel in time.

Although disappointed not to have gotten a close-up, still he'd seen himself on the silver screen, and how many can say that?

18.

FRIDAY AFTER LABOR DAY was Jeff's 14th birthday and his first day at Garrett Prep. Prep's bus not beginning until Monday, Gerald's mother drove the boys to school, Carol in the other front seat of Ruth's white Mustang to learn the route. The three boys sat in the backseat, thighs touching warmly.

After a summer spent outdoors but inside his own head, Jeff felt relief at facing something new—ready to learn, ready to study. School would run from homeroom at 8:45 a.m. to the buses' departure when the chapel bells rang the quarter-hour at 4:45 p.m. He wore a sport coat of bilious green his mother chose but, having inherited his father's tie collection, enlivened it with Dent's favorite stripes.

The drive took 20 minutes out Veirs Mill Road, rounding through the enclave of Garrett Park before emerging beneath a Georgian brick monolith that commanded a hundred hilltop acres. A smokestack and the chapel's bell tower flanked the main building. Unseen behind it were the old and new gyms.

— *THE HOLY HUGS OF FATHER S.* —

It was, as it was meant to be, an intimidating sight. From the portico, a regular cadence of tall windows on either side led to outsized wings. The cupola's lantern stood tall over everything.

At the top of a driveway that climbed alongside golf-course fairways, Ruth pointed out Ethel Kennedy at the wheel of a Pontiac convertible, letting off one of her boys.

Jeff followed Gerald and Vance up the steps into the foyer. A bronze table stood square in the center of the terrazzo floor, and a double staircase opposite flowed beneath a huge stained-glass window. He was dismayed to find his summer friend Gerald transformed into an altogether different person, hailing classmates and smashing them on the back as everybody went out to the terrace in the rear. There milled the entire student body of 320 boys.

For twenty minutes they mixed and milled, and Jeff tried to be one of them. But he was unnerved to find how rusty he was at any kind of sociability—rusting since school let out, like everybody else, of course, but really since his father died. Though he introduced himself, he rapidly found that sophomores and above didn't care to know him, nor did 8th graders (for the first time, Prep had no 7th grade), and even among the freshmen the only ones who cared were those also in Dr. Lister's homeroom.

And everybody knew each other, anyway. In fact, Jeff was one of only three new members of the freshman class, everyone else having attended Prep's 8th grade. That Joe Kennedy wasn't invited back (oh, the stories about rascally Joe!) had opened up one of those places.

The crowd was loud, joshing, mocking, boys vying to be seen, orbiting old leaders, trying to work out the updated hierarchy, everybody in dynamic transition to his next avatar. Status ruled; that ineffable quality filled the air. Jeff thought if a scientific instrument could read the waves of *status* swirling around them it would be as revealing as an infrared look at the stars. Possibly such a device would more easily detect the anxiety attending its lack.

It struck him that his fellow students, all of them sons of successful fathers, men of respect, didn't want to be themselves at all—they wanted to *be* their fathers. Any difference between themselves and their Dads they perceived as a shortcoming, a deviation. And anything of no immediate use to that reduplication was to be avoided or discarded. They were at Prep to learn the shortest possible route to replicating that paternal success.

Jeff had loved his father, but had no particular wish to *be* him.

Then a redfaced priest—Father Dooley, drill sergeant to generations—barked a stentorian order and everybody hurried indoors to find his homeroom.

Jeff followed Gerald and Vance downstairs to the freshman homerooms in the north wing's basement. Dark and gloomy, it was floored in linoleum on concrete, with asbestos-wrapped pipes crisscrossing just overhead. The windows opened to graveled wells. A partition closed off Jeff's classroom from Gerald's; Vance's was across the way. Everything was tired and dreary, even unto green chalkboards that tended to refuse new chalk, deeming sufficient what they'd shown for 50 years past.

Twenty-five boys—including one of the school's three Black students—filed into Dr. Lister's homeroom. Chairs with Formica desktops braced by arms sat five across and five deep. Dr. Lister assigning them alphabetically, Jeff found himself in the second row from the door, four seats back.

Following homeroom announcements, Dr. Lister — who like the other lay teachers wore academic robes — started his History of Western Civilization lesson by reading the textbook aloud from the beginning with the boys following along. Turning the page, Jeff was startled and entranced by the drawing spread over two pages: a busy view of Greek male athletes competing in the nude. Its most surprising — even compelling — feature was that, despite a plethora of young buttocks on display (pert, tight) and a multitude of flexed backs, shapely arms, legs and flowing locks, no genitals could be seen — no, not one cock. Anywhere one's eye would expect to find one — innocently directed by the composition's sinuous lines — was blocked by someone's discus or javelin, thwarting it of seeing what it expected to see. Both the result and the intent fascinated Jeff. Such a very Roman Catholic tease.

Dr. Lister droned on, except when, looking embarrassed, he improvised some not very germane remark.

The next class was English. Jeff had read the books on Mr. Finian's summer reading list — one of the few who had, a show of hands revealed — but Mr. Finian said they wouldn't be studying them anyway. Sturdy, bald and short, he had a tendency to rise to the tips of his toes in chasing his voice to upper registers of indignation. Today, flat-footed, he told of his July adventure, driving a Corvette Sting-Ray at top speed, courtesy of former students. "They were surprised I could do it," he sniffed. Then, rising several inches, he gave a shrill preview of his outrage at the Chinese Cultural Revolution, which he foresaw engulfing

America next.

After English came a break when the student store down the hall opened up to sell Pepsi, Hershey bars, pens and pencils.

The last class before lunch was Latin, taught by Father Brody. Tall, his belly swelling his cassock and a goofy smile playing beneath his glasses, he drilled them on the first declension.

Lunch was served freshmen and 8th graders together in the festive, light-filled south-wing dining room. Two boys at each table laid with white tablecloths and heavy queensware were seconded to carry serving trays out from the kitchen, dishes then to be passed from hand to hand. WINX played softly on the P.A. as a fountain plashed.

Father Dooley patrolled the room enforcing silence. Hearing whispers, he grew redder and redder as he hunted their source until, catching a miscreant in the act, his arm shot out: *"Jug!"*

That left only the fountain and the chink of forks against china, to a subdued *Eleanor Rigby*.

In the afternoon came Algebra, Religion and Public Speaking.

Then it was time for sports. Gerald had told Jeff—and Vance confirmed—what the catalog never said, that students were expected to "go out" for sports (Prep's devotion partly based on the dubious premise that sports prevent boys from masturbating). Jeff had no wish to "go out" for the football team, basketball team, track team, wrestling team, swim team or any other kind of team, so went to the library instead.

He liked the library. Its reading room was carpeted and well-lit, with tables and comfortable chairs, walls lined by book shelves, more serving as dividers. He recognized an 8th grader, Robert F. Kennedy, Jr., reading a magazine. His father had sent a note when Jeff's died.

Choosing *Is Paris Burning?* Jeff was immersed—until a hand clamped his shoulder.

"Basketball, *now*," barked a novitiate in a sweatsuit.

Jeff and others dragooned by Mr. Beach (including RFK, Jr.) were led down the corridor past photographs of boys rigidly posing—*Class of 1957, Class of 1944, Class of 1930, Class of 1919*—downstairs and out a loading dock to a court of broken blacktop near the heating plant and pro shop, where other prisoners waited. Mr. Beach had everybody shed their jackets, divided them into teams, told Jeff's to take off their shirts and whistled them into—despite his moving through them a human tornado, determined to jumpstart them—the most anemic intramural game of shirts and skins ever played.

When the Jesuit finally whistled it to a close, Jeff could put his shirt and coat back on, pick up his books and, with Gerald and Vance, go find his mother, waiting in front of Ethel Kennedy's convertible.

Carol asked how his first day had gone.

"All right," said Jeff.

That evening she took him to the Hot Shoppe to celebrate.

MONDAY MORNING, Carol dropped the three boys on Georgia Avenue between Howard Johnson's and the Ford dealership. Prep's bus would rumble along at 8:15 or so to make its final pick-up.

While they stood peering up the street, Gerald

identified the far horizon's bump as Sugarloaf Mountain.

The bus's new Georgia Avenue dogleg—previously, Ruth had driven her son and Vance the whole way to school—necessitated unconscionably early pick-up times in Northwest, Chevy Chase and Bethesda. And not only were the three schedule-disruptors picked up last in the morning, in the evening they got dropped off *first*, a little after 5:00.

Naturally the other boys resented the change, and expressed it, too, blaming not their old friends Gerald and Vance, but the new boy. Jeff pointed out that it wasn't his fault; pointed it out every day.

In homeroom Dr. Lister took attendance—his harried air expressing a wish to be elsewhere—before reading on in Western Civ, while Jeff studied his naked, emasculated athletes.

In English class, taking his stance at the rear of the room, Mr. Finian called on various boys to read Shelley and Keats, including Randy, above whose desk he hovered. Randy was a dedicated athlete, but his voice hadn't changed yet and he read *Ozymandias* in high piping tones:

Look on my Works, ye Mighty, and despair!

Jeff's peripheral vision caught something he'd never seen before—a teacher undoing a student's shirt buttons. Turning to look full on, he saw Mr. Finian concentrating on the book he held in his left hand while his right hand, seemingly of itself, delved into Randy's chest. The boy's face raged red as Mr. Finian tweaked a nipple, then, still fondling him, called on another student.

—THE HOLY HUGS OF FATHER S.—

Then he was at the front of the class on the tips of his toes denouncing Chairman Mao.

In Latin Father Brody, standing above the biggest student, Woodrow, right in the front row, was drilling the class on the first declension when he put *his* hand into *Woodrow's* shirt. Woodrow blushed furiously. In the room's odd atmosphere, Jeff detected dismay, *fear*, above all *gladness* at not being thus singled out. Woodrow's distress he could only guess at. Meanwhile Father Brody took out his hand to turn the page and replaced it in Woodrow's breast, his face as unconcerned doing what he was doing as Mr. Finian's had been.

Soon he moved on to a boy with a perfect Roman nose and, stooping, slipped fingers into *his* shirt.

No one said anything, then or later. No boy *not* fondled in class wished to rock that particular boat, nor did any boy who *was* fondled want any allusion made to it. Jeff wondered whether he should say something or tell someone, but he didn't. Like everybody else he pushed the sight into a memory sink.

After lunch came his first gym class. He was nervous about changing into his jockstrap, gym shorts and T-shirt — he'd never taken off his clothes in company with others before — but figured that what others could do, he could do, too. And was curious besides.

When the time came he stripped off efficiently at a bench in the big locker room beneath the main gym. Amidst the hubbub, he noticed myriad glances shooting everywhere. His own yielded the interesting fact that boys of 14 present different stages of development — some bare of pubic hair, others hairy as men. One cute classmate stood with his back to his locker, taking off his clothes as sensuously as Michelangelo's *Slave* while looking around like a kid on Christmas morning.

Clanging his locker shut, Jeff headed upstairs, where Coach Tweedy named two captains to choose sides for basketball—Jeff chosen early, for his height (it didn't happen again).

At the whistle, everybody clambered downstairs to the locker room.

Jeff stripped off, grabbed a towel and padded to the showers—the second one in there, beaten only by Henry Keating, the handsomest boy he'd ever seen. In class Henry sat to Jeff's right, his comely head within the peripheral vision Jeff swore by.

Jeff politely positioned himself as far away as possible, but they looked at each other until other boys came in and steamed up the room, revolving beneath the spray, looking around avidly. Jeff was surprised at just how avidly the boys gawked at one another's bodies. The Senator's son who sat behind him in class stood with hands on hips candidly assessing chests, asses and dark-nestled cocks. Jeff wanted to gawk, too, but feared he didn't share the general license to do so.

Grabbing his towel, he dried off and got dressed. It hadn't been so bad.

At the end of the class day—signaled by Father Dooley snarling over the P.A. the names of those condemned to *Jug*—Jeff again took refuge in the library.

He was studying Antietam battlefield photographs when Mr. Beach shook his shoulder.

"Basketball, *now*."

19.

FATHER SCHMIDT TOLD Father Robin about seeing *We Are Christ* at St. Jude's (though neglecting to say, through the windows), and praised it as an effective showcase for his choir.

In response Father Robin decided to sponsor a showing himself. He procured a print from the National Liturgical Council to project in his parish hall and invited Father Schmidt as guest of honor, and also to stay the night.

When the evening came, Father Schmidt nudged his Fury behind the trees and parked next to the MG. Though St. Martin's was only marginally more prosperous than St. Datian's, Father Robin had lately managed to build a new rectory. Screened by trees, its terrace surrounded walls mostly of glass. Wearing a bright, open-necked shirt and trailed by a handsome, mop-haired youth, he came out to greet Father Schmidt.

"Hey, Father," he called, "glad you could make it."

"Thanks, Father," said Father Schmidt, eyeing the kid hanging behind his host.

"This is Brett," said Father Robin. "He's all excited

about your movie. Wanted to meet you."

"Hardly my movie," Father said modestly.

"Cooking outdoors. Hope you don't mind, my Sodality's come to help? Half a dozen boys. You'll like them. I'm sure vocations are rattling around in some of them. Right, Brett? Interested in the priesthood? Or at least in getting holy hugs from priests?"

"Yes, Father."

Brett showed Father Schmidt to the guest room where he was to sleep. Its sliders gave a vision of woods. Then he took him outdoors, found him a Michelob and introduced him to the Sodality, sociable lads of about 16—that most devout age.

"Don't know how many will come to the screening," Father Robin said as he grilled steaks. "It's Friday, even down here there's competition. But there's a lot of interest in the new liturgy—if not overmuch enthusiasm. In the cradle of the American Church?"

"I miss the Latin myself," said Father Schmidt. "Historic and—forgive my saying—*fast*. But here we are."

"Here we are," sighed Father Robin. "If the Church is becoming more open I'm sure that's a good thing. Even if it turns out no one actually wants to see how the sausage is made." He raised his beer: *"To Holy Mother Church!"*

"Holy Mother Church!" echoed the Sodality.

After dinner families began to arrive next door, headed by stalwart women in hats accompanied by less eager-looking husbands and children.

Father Robin greeted them, his guest at his side.

"Evening, Mrs. Walker, good to see you and your strapping boys. This is Father Schmidt, the star of our show this evening."

—THE HOLY HUGS OF FATHER S.—

"Hardly the star," said Father.

But he was glad to see *We Are Christ* indoors. He sat on the aisle halfway back, Brett next to him, leaning into him, his thigh warm against Father's, his knee knocking Father's at moments of enthusiasm. The film again struck him as professional and not unentertaining. Accompanied by a bouncy score, the young people went through their liturgy-enhanced days and Monsignor said Mass to enthusiastic response, Father Schmidt's choir visible and audible.

Just listen to that choir! he thought. *And tell me again why I'm stuck in the sticks!*

OK, so I sinned, but I confessed and did my penance, didn't I? Not that I did any harm anyway — I never *would! So tell me: Why am I stuck in the sticks?*

Well, know what? If this is where I have to be, OK, fine — but I might as well get some fun out of it!

He pressed his knee against Brett's.

The lights came up to lively applause, and compliments flew, particularly about the choir. Was something similar in store for St. Datian's?

Not sure yet, said Father; it depended.

Back at the rectory, while the Sodality unrolled sleeping bags on the living room floor or in Father Robin's room, Brett came into Father Schmidt's to make sure he had everything he needed, and smiled when Father closed the door and kissed him.

After a night knock-knock-knocking at heaven's door, Father felt *good* in the morning, and *vindicated*. Brett stowed his suitcase in the Fury for him and hugged him tight.

Before Father left, Father Robin invited him to join himself "and a few priest friends" the following week at the Eastern Shore cottage one had near Ocean City where they liked to unwind from their weekends.

Father Schmidt asked if Brett would be there?

"You never can tell with that one," answered Father Robin.

In the event Brett couldn't make it, but Father Schmidt didn't miss him, not with the equally young and willing Michael to play with. Four priests and four youngsters stayed two nights at the cottage, enjoying good fellowship and absolving one another's sins as fast as they could commit them.

Father Robin also talked up *We Are Christ*, with the result that—after arranging for fill-ins by other priests—the group made an overnight trip to the Anne Arundel County rectory of one to catch the Sunday morning TV broadcast.

By now the film seemed to Father Schmidt lapidary, *classic,* even on a small screen with chamfered corners.

20.

IN ONE REGARD Jeff improved his lot at Prep. There was no evading Mr. Beach in the library after classes, so he took to stalking the golf course with a sophomore fellow refugee instead.

But watching foursomes pass, particularly the pro and the team he coached, inspired him. One day he hauled Dent's clubs to school on the bus and signed up for lessons. They and his practice rounds began to absorb the time after classes.

And he took to the game. At nearly six feet two, despite being yet only 146 lbs., his frame had enough power to drive the ball, nor was accuracy in question—he was reminded of his cellist aunt who boasted *"the vibrato is built in."* And the challenge of sinking it, however comical, was satisfying. It was the perfect game for a high schooler with time to kill. Soon he went out for the golf team.

The third hole was his favorite, a challenging par 4 190 yards, an uphill drive over a hidden water hazard, with a pivot towards the green. The drive had to be judged just right. He loved lofting the cup's silly pennant.

Jeff marveled at how different from his fecund walks along Northwest Branch playing the course was. Instead of helping him feel at one with Nature and her cycle of bursting jungle growth and ensuing decomposition, from every standpoint the course, driving range and putting green represented control, or an attempt at it. But for a kid always scared by his Church's beloved *"forever and ever,"* it allowed him at last to accept eternity, as being the only span of time sufficient for the game of golf.

He began to enjoy his afternoons. Returning to the pro shop after a circuit tragic or triumphant, he surveyed the school's Georgian power architecture with equanimity; *not* intimidating viewed 9-iron in hand. For a few minutes he might josh with his teammates while looking on pityingly at Mr. Beach's zombies—Mr. Beach corkscrewing through them, a veritable cyclone—then go catch his bus.

JEFF ALSO DEVELOPED—or discovered, for it felt as though it had been there all along, awaiting merely the boy's appearance in person—a crush on Henry Keating.

His sculpted good looks, brown-eyed and dark-haired— Oh, Henry's perfection, his grace, his brightness, his propinquity (just one row over!) made Jeff feel privileged to breathe the same air, if unworthy to walk the same Earth.

He felt this even while having a dim sense that a crush can't be love because it's one-sided. It *felt* like love. He was aware of him every moment until, after classes, Henry went off to junior-varsity football practice. At night Jeff revolved through the day's Henry sightings, every word heard, every action observed. But though he felt saturated in longing for him, he was unable to picture Henry in a sexual situation. Taking himself in hand in bed—for the first time in months—got him nowhere; he *couldn't* sully Henry's image thus, *couldn't* inflict his guilt on him.

It didn't occur to him that Henry, a boarder also new to Prep, might be lonely. Instead, shame had Jeff avoiding him as best he could, and thus he missed signs that Henry felt friendly towards him. One day they walked downstairs, Henry behind him with his hand clamping his shoulder (Jeff gave him a nervous smile). Another time, retrieving books from beneath their desks, they bumped heads and laughed. As the really good-looking always are, Henry was popular, but in fact—despite being a JV punter—he fit in imperfectly with the jocks who ran the school. But speech was impossible for Jeff.

School otherwise continued dreary. Inducements to learning were paltry, to enjoyment nil. Dr. Lister's rambling lectures failed to allay his own boredom, but stories about World War II Istanbul—his obituary years later spoke of his work in Allied intelligence there—went untold. Latin was a black hole of drills, Algebra a waste, Religion dismal and Public Speaking farcical, save for the teacher's unexpected penchant for showing Buster Keaton movies.

Mr. Finian's English class Jeff enjoyed, however, even if any allusion to the Red Guards (and such allusions by his students abounded) put Mr. Finian on his toes, quivering and incensed. One day he escorted a Taiwanese delegation to every classroom; Jeff never saw harder-looking men.

Mr. Finian also continued to stick his hand into boys' shirts. He had his favorites—Paulson, of the Roman nose; little Randy; big Woodrow, who, almost as tall sitting as

Mr. Finian standing, meekly submitted as the teacher undid buttons while raising his voice to divert everybody from what he was doing in front of their faces.

Then he found a new victim. One morning he had Henry Keating recite *Danny Deever* at his seat and meanwhile thrust a hand down his shirt. Henry's voice became husky. Even as his fingers moved across his chest, Mr. Finian led a discussion of the poem, before finally withdrawing his hand with a nod, as if to say, "You can button up now."

Father Brody soon zeroed in on Henry, too. Henry would slump to make the priest double over to work his fingers in between buttons, but didn't protest. Did the predators compare notes? They must have. Meanwhile no one said anything, *ever;* not in class, not between classes, not after class. The closest—but not very close—approach was gossip about Mr. Finian's supposedly living with a man. Jeff thought Mr. Finian might just as well have taken out his penis and beat off in Ricky's face, or Father Brody push his into Henry's mouth: No one would have said a word.

One Monday morning Father Brody entered the classroom and piled his books on the table.

"Saw you on the bus Saturday, Henry. Oh, did you have those girls hot and bothered. They went, 'Oh, Henry! Oh, *Henry!*' Just like you were a candy bar."

The class laughed.

Jeff asked himself what he would do if Mr. Finian or Father Brody stuck a hand down *his* shirt?

Then wondered why they hadn't. Wasn't he attractive enough? Or did he bear the stigmata of the abused? (Except shouldn't they find that enticing?)

— *THE HOLY HUGS OF FATHER S.* —

How did the fondled boys feel? Did Henry want to talk about it? Jeff didn't ask.

PREP'S FRESHMAN RELIGION teacher was young Father Mooney. Taking Religion with Father Mooney struck Jeff as being not unlike studying tax accounting or law: There seemed no end to the shifts or shadings, allowances or dodges to be found in the ancient art of theology. He liked the textbook, though, full of bright, simplified Bible scenes, colors separated by lines as in stained glass windows; very Vatican II.

One day Father Mooney asked Jeff to come by his residence upstairs after classes.

Hoping not to be late for golf, Jeff set off promptly down the terrazzo, hearing his footsteps echo. Opposite Father Mooney lived Prep's organist and resident exotic, Brother Ralph, an ancient married man who by Papal dispensation entered the Jesuits the same day in 1921 his wife entered a convent in Virginia.

Jeff knocked on Father Mooney's door. Opening it to a snug living room, the priest smiled at him from a bathrobe. His hair was tousled and wet.

"Ah, Jeff, come in. Have a seat. Like a Coke?"

"Thank you."

Indicating the couch, Father Mooney poured Cokes, handed Jeff one and, saying, "Please excuse me," stepped into the bathroom to make a pass at his head with a towel and brush his hair. Coming out, he sat down next to Jeff, who wasn't at all certain there was anything beneath that robe.

Eyes bright, the priest unnecessarily explained, "Just

showered."

"Ah."

"Thanks for coming up, Jeff. What I wanted to talk to you about— Well, as a teacher of Religion, I try to be sensitive as to whether any of my students might have a religious vocation. And it occurs to me that just possibly *you* might have one."

At *you* Father Mooney tapped Jeff's knee.

"You're putting me on!" said Jeff. Never did a phrase more artificial-sounding to his own ears escape him.

"Anything I can do to help," said the priest, opening his legs. "When I was your age—"

"Thanks," said Jeff, "but it's hard to think I'd have a vocation when I don't believe in God."

It was the first time he'd said it.

Startled, Father Mooney asked, "How's that?"

"Don't you think God's a story meant for children, like Santa Claus? When decent people around the world believe in such different things?"

"Ah, you're so cosmopolitan!" said the priest, smoothing his hair. The gesture lifted his robe from his thighs and Jeff could just about see— "You're going?"

Jeff had come to his feet.

"Golf," he explained. "Thanks for the Coke, Father."

He saw himself out.

That day's nine holes gave him his best score yet.

ONE FRIDAY EVENING Ruth drove her son and Jeff back to campus for the homecoming dance.

The evening of his first dance at St. Jude's, after dressing with care and combing a modicum of Vitalis into his hair, Jeff—agonizingly self-conscious—asked his mother, "Do I look handsome?"

"*We-ell,*" Carol said punctiliously, "you look *good.*"

Prep's gym was decorated with balloons and streamers and patrolled by Jesuits. A rudimentary lightshow of rotating colored gels played over the room, and in the announcer's roost a turntable was plugged into the P.A. Lights down, music up—rock and R&B—the floor rapidly filled with boys in sport coats and girls in party dresses.

Jeff and Gerald hung near each other, dancing with sweet girls from Holton Arms and St. Abigail's whose names they never learned. Jeff's focus was elsewhere—on Henry Keating in a dinner jacket looking as if he knew exactly what he was doing, his heel *pounding pounding pounding* to the Monkees' *Last Train to Clarksville.* The girls certainly liked him.

But home in bed, Jeff still couldn't do anything with Henry. Reverting to an old standby, he fantasized they shared a tent. It didn't work, save to inform him how pathetic in their nature sexual fantasies are.

So he developed a new, non-sexual one. Remembering a scene from a long-canceled TV show—*1, 2, 3 Go!*—that had an English boy save young Richard Thomas by pulling him back as he started across a London street looking the wrong way, Jeff imagined shoving Henry out of the path of a speeding car (he had in mind the cream-colored Cougar a senior drove), but being himself slammed to the pavement.

"I'm OK, I'm OK," he would gasp to his new best friend.

21.

EVERY AUTUMN Monsignor Brannick visited his beloved ancestral homeland for a week, along with eight or ten parishioners who chipped in on his first-class airfare, hotel rooms and meals. Always they rented a coach to explore the countryside, especially County Cork, whence Monsignor's grandparents emigrated, and always he came home raving about the beauty of the young Irish.

But this year the rigors of breaking in a new auxiliary delayed his trip. Not until nearly Thanksgiving did the grapevine inform Father Schmidt that Monsignor was about to embark.

Arranging for a friend of Father Robin's to stand in for him at St. Datian's, Father told him that should anything come up, he could be reached at St. Jude's.

Father Robin advised against the plan: You can't go back, he urged, especially when you're beginning to settle in. But Father's nostalgia for St. Jude's was acute.

Lightheartedly tossing his suitcase into the Fury's trunk Monday morning (Monsignor's trips always ran Sunday-to-Sunday) Father Schmidt drove north. The sunlight's flattened angle, the bare trees and harvested fields proclaimed summertime over. No veils of overhanging boughs ushered him from the *Ark* and the *Dove* to modern times, but the roads through St. Mary's County, Calvert County, Anne Arundel County, Charles County, Prince George's County into Montgomery County were empty as ever, the Confederate-looking sentry as lonely, Confederate flags more tattered.

He had to endure an hour's static before the radio suddenly blurted *Winchester Cathedral* (very appropriate).

His expression priestly, Father navigated familiar turf along Colesville Road and University Boulevard, finally pulling up behind St. Jude's new rectory between Monsignor's Grand Prix and Father Heath's Bug.

Carrying his suitcase over the terrace—a marble Mary blessing him—to the double doors, Father knocked showily and went inside. He felt at home immediately.

Mrs. Logan came out of the kitchen exclaiming and hugged him tight; he always was her favorite. Father Heath hurried downstairs to see what the commotion was.

"Father Schmidt! What are you doing here?"

"Didn't Monsignor tell you? Staying the week. Thought you might want help with the Masses?"

"Always," said Father Heath, adding, as Father hauled his suitcase upstairs, "About to have lunch."

"Be right down," Father called, going into the suite overlooking playground and school and claiming the bed with his suitcase.

Downstairs, he asked, "How are you finding things, Father?"

"Fine, Father. Really good parish, really fine people."

"My choir still going?"

"Oh yes, Mr. Grimes is devoted."

Mrs. Logan, flustered by Father's return, served up the soup and hurriedly made more sandwiches.

After lunch, Father Schmidt lay down to the happy sounds of children at recess. He reveled in the suite. A walnut-encased color TV was aimed at the bed, but he imagined that, as a guest, he should join Father Heath downstairs in the living room evenings, if that was where he watched TV.

At least no one would have to see Monsignor's programs or endure his bared gums as he guffawed at *Gilligan's Island* or *The Beverly Hillbillies*.

Visiting that afternoon's choir practice, Father was beseeched by Mr. Grimes to lead it. Mr. Grimes was at his wit's end, missing work to lead practices and frantically casting around for another solution. Father complimented his handling of the choir, because it costs nothing to be nice, but privately was dismayed at its raggedness. But there was nothing he could do about it, save give it some good practices himself.

Then Father drove out to the Osbornes'.

Carol opened the door, surprised and pleased. "Father Schmidt!"

A few minutes later they were in the living room, sipping gin-and-tonics.

"Jeff won't be home for a while, Father. I have to meet his bus in Wheaton."

"How's he doing? How's he like Garrett Prep? I haven't seen him since the incident at St. Datian's."

"Incident?"

"When he fell into the open grave?"

"Open *grave?*"

—THE HOLY HUGS OF FATHER S.—

"He didn't tell you? Well, he wasn't hurt, just shaken up. The boys were playing tag after dinner and—*boom!*"

"Poor kid. But he's doing fine, Father. Likes Garrett Prep. He's on the golf team."

"I'm so glad."

She pressed him to stay for dinner, so he used her phone to call the rectory.

When it was time to go meet Jeff's bus, they got in the Mustang.

"Three big boys," Carol said, starting the engine, "but some days the Lincoln's just too big to drive."

She put the car into reverse and pressed the accelerator. The engine revved, but the car didn't move.

She slapped the gearshift to neutral, back to reverse and revved.

Nothing happened.

All she could do was try again and again, double-check that the parking brake was off, read the gear knob's diagram to make sure it matched her muscle memory.

"I don't know what the hell's going on, Father."

Upset, even undone—hair springing up, dress coming off one shoulder—she got out and slammed the door.

"May I?" asked Father.

Getting behind the wheel, he put the car in gear, pressed the accelerator, went nowhere.

He asked for a flashlight and a towel.

She brought them and, handing her his jacket and lying on the towel, Father Schmidt pulled himself under the car.

Carol heard, "*Aha!*"

Suppressing a smile, he pulled himself out from under.

"Carol, you won't believe this, but the driveshaft's missing."

"The *driveshaft's* missing?"

"I'd call the police if I were you. *Somebody* took it. If you want, I can pick up the boys."

"Thanks, Father. Thank you very much."

She told him where the bus dropped them.

Pulling the Fury into HoJo's parking lot and seeing boys in jackets and ties standing at a loss, Father honked. All three turned. Two stared blankly while—to his dismay—Jeff turned away.

Father rolled down his window and called, "Jeff, your Mom sent me."

They got in the car then, Jeff and Vance in back, the looker called Gerald in front (*"Ten!"* Father Schmidt could hear Father Robin breathe). Father explained the driveshaft situation while he drove, at right turns glancing down at Gerald's crotch; *something* was going on in there.

Directed to Vance's house, then Gerald's, he dropped them off. Jeff stayed in the backseat as they rounded the curves of Storybook Forest back towards his house. He hadn't said a word.

"Jeff," Father asked, peering into the rearview, "you're not *mad* at me, are you?"

"Let me off, please, Father."

"Can't let you off *here,* Jeff. Look, I'd hate to think you were *mad* at me."

Pushing on the front seatback, Jeff reached for the door handle.

"Whoa!" said Father, braking.

Jeff scrambled out and slammed the door.

Nothing Father could do but drive on.

A patrol car sat in the Osbornes' driveway and policemen flanked Carol. As Father came up one was saying, "Well, but if you *were* driving the Mustang, Mrs. Osborne, we'd have to arrest you."

"Can't drink and drive, Ma'am," said the other.

"But— But—" She was indignant.

Father reached a hand to her shoulder.

"Didn't drive an inch," he said lightly. *"Couldn't."*

"Believe it or not, Ma'am, we've had Mustang driveshafts stolen lately. Must be a demand. You should call your insurance company."

The police were leaving as Jeff walked up. While he went downstairs to change clothes Carol called the Ford dealership.

When he came upstairs to where Father and Carol were having G&Ts, his mother asked, "How was school, honey?"

"Fine," he said.

They ate at the kitchen table—cheeseburgers grilled in the electric frypan. Father said grace.

"Everybody misses you, Father," said Carol. "But it must be wonderful having your own parish."

"Oh yes," said Father, and asked Jeff how he liked Latin ("Fine") and golf ("Fine").

"May I be excused?" Jeff asked before dessert. He went downstairs.

When Carol apologized for him, Father told her, "I was like that at his age. I'll just go talk to him."

Downstairs, he knocked on the door.

"Jeff? It's Father."

"Go away."

"Just want to talk. I think there must be some misunderstanding. . . Jeff? Won't you let me in?"

So reasonable! He knocked on the hollow, resounding

door, *knocked knocked knocked,* but Jeff refused to open it or say a word.

Upstairs, upset, Father reported his failure to Carol over ice cream, thanked her for dinner and drove back to the rectory. He couldn't remember why he'd come or what he'd hoped to accomplish.

Father Heath was upstairs in his own suite, so Father Schmidt went to his and lay down to watch *The Andy Griffith Show.*

The next morning, Father said 7:00 a.m. Mass (as he did every day that week, capably served by an 8th grader), and afterwards Mrs. Logan gave him a full English breakfast.

In the evenings he reveled in the luxury of his suite's TV reception. Sometimes you don't value what you have until you've lost it. In Bullnose he could pull in Annapolis stations only in a stiff east wind.

He also enjoyed getting to know Father Heath, who reminded him of himself when he was new: *idealistic.* He yearned to pass on some shortcuts and workarounds, but Father Heath in his bright-eyed fashion seemed intent on doing things the very hardest way possible, and to find satisfaction in it, too. So Father let him be.

Saturday night he was sprawled in bed watching *Mission: Impossible,* heavily aware that he'd have to find out the next morning at just what hour of afternoon or evening Monsignor would be dropped off so he could get out of Dodge first.

But hardly had *Mission: Impossible*'s tape sizzled in auto-immolation than voices rang out downstairs.

Getting up and cracking his door, Father was horrified to hear "—always an hour longer flying west, I'll feel it tomorrow, but it was a good trip. Oh, the beauty of young

Irish lasses! Angels! Everything all right here?"

"Let me help," said Father Heath, starting up the stairs with Monsignor's heaviest bags. "Everything's fine. Father Schmidt's been a godsend, taking early Mass—"

"Father *Schmidt?*" Monsignor asked in astonishment behind him, a bag in one hand and souvenir shillelagh in the other.

"Yes, he's just up here," said Father Heath, suddenly sounding nervous.

"Father Schmidt!" Monsignor roared from the top of the staircase.

In pajamas Father stepped into the hallway.

"Monsignor?"

"You will kindly take yourself home to your own parish this *instant!"*

"If you'll permit me, I'm already in bed—"

Monsignor hefted the shillelagh. "You cost me my *hat,* goddam it!"

"All right, all right, I'm going," Father said. "No need for that."

He pulled clothes on over his pajamas and threw everything into his suitcase while Monsignor continued to rave.

"And coming back under false pretenses? Taking advantage of Father Heath? Mrs. Logan, too? *Underhanded!* And just to spell it out for you, Father—since I know your tendency towards equivocation—underhandedness is a *sin."*

"Told you, I'm going, I'm going."

He clumped downstairs, slammed the door behind him and came out of the drive gunning the Fury.

Father Schmidt drove south in the night, recurring

again and again to the fraught scene just past.

But he happened to think, too, of the delicious period following Pope John XXIII's death three years earlier: Papal appointments lapsing until a new Pope confirmed them, Monsignor Brannick reverted for months to being plain Father Brannick in an ordinary black cassock. Father Schmidt had taken unholy delight in rubbing it in.

He drove through Montgomery County, Prince George's County, Charles County, Anne Arundel County, Calvert County into St. Mary's County. It still felt like driving into the past, but—to his surprise—he found himself thinking that at least the past doesn't change, it's solid and secure, you know where you are and what to expect.

Maybe St. Datian's was the place for him?

Home at last, he faced the nuisance of sleeping the rest of the night in his lumpy guest bed, the priest filling in for him being asleep in his.

22.

Coach Tweedy announced a schoolwide round-robin wrestling tournament. Boys would be paired off with others of their weight class in gym, each bout's winner to wrestle other winners, until the homeroom champs faced one another in matches to be held in front of the assembled student body. The excitement!

Gerald happened to be a JV wrestler who fought daily battles to get his weight down to the next lower class. He spent extra hours in the steam room, triumphing at every ounce lost.

Jeff saw who his weight-class rivals were—one was Henry Keating—and prepared to maneuver his way through them. He had no intention of making a spectacle of himself in front of the whole school.

Per his plan, he won his first bout, though such close contract with that particular classmate repelled him. But accidentally he won his second one, too. So he *had* to throw the third, where his opponent happened to be (at 147 lbs.) Henry Keating, who'd also won a couple of bouts.

Jeff encountered two difficulties in theirs. The first was his conviction that Henry, too, was trying to throw it.

The second was merely a matter of Nature.

As classmates around the mat yelled encouragement, Jeff discovered that, however attentive he was to dramatizing his defeat, of appearing to be crushed and outmaneuvered, Henry was doing the same. Also he was finding the encounter highly erotic. Legs intertwined, arms and shoulders straining, for long moments they lay against each other in embraces that felt like lovemaking, Jeff consumedly aware of how good Henry smelled, how intimate his face seen an inch away. Every muscle distended, he was hard, and so was Henry.

Classmates continued to shout advice. Only Coach Tweedy looked on with a skeptical expression, as though there was something he wanted to say. But he didn't say it.

Finally, in a panic, on the verge of coming, Jeff with a mighty groan succeeded in throwing himself under Henry and pressing his own shoulders to the mat.

They panted grinning into each other's faces before Henry's arm was held aloft — the winner! Jeff sprang up, carrying himself carefully, but finding that his jockstrap canted his erection to the side. Henry — boys clapping him on the back — strategically employed a towel while accepting congratulations.

Later that week Jeff had the pleasure of joining the rest of the school on the bleachers to watch the tournament of champions, which preempted an afternoon's sports.

It began with lower weight classes. RFK, Jr. was pinned handily. Later, to groans and thumps, cheers and jeers, Henry Keating lost to Gerald. Watching, Jeff realized he might have survived wrestling under the collective gaze.

—THE HOLY HUGS OF FATHER S.—

A few minutes later, hair damp from the showers, Henry joined his classmates, pushing along the bleachers and, with a hand to Jeff's shoulder, making him scooch over. Jeff colored. Easier to fantasize about saving Henry's life than to chat with him or smile. So he ignored him.

But he realized how strange his sitting frozen must strike Henry. *Losing patience with you,* he told himself. *Sympathy, too. Just turn your head and say Congratulations.*

But guilt and shame crushed any natural behavior, made it impossible to turn his head and say *anything*. Henry Keating couldn't possibly like *Jeff*. If he knew about Jeff and Father Schmidt, he'd be *disgusted,* and rightly so.

Matches finished, the boys were released, Jeff to go home, Henry to return to his dorm.

But Jeff finally made progress in his bedtime fantasies. For weeks, he'd gotten nowhere, but now he needed simply to recall lying against Henry, pushing, to get going reliably.

Meanwhile, the golf course closed down for winter, leaving Jeff again vulnerable after classes. He'd slip into the library, but soon Mr. Beach would stride in in sweats: "Basketball, *now!*"

And once again Jeff would be moving in the slow, sad choreography of the uninterested, sonambulistically trying to avoid the Kryptonite ball.

23.

CHRISTMAS FALLING ON Sunday that year, Prep's classes were to end the preceding Wednesday. Its annual Bacchanal would take place that afternoon, and Thursday morning boarders would be shuttled to the airports and Union Station. Classes would resume January 8, making for a thumping two-and-a-half-week break.

The only drawback was that the teachers gave heavy assignments; Mr. Finian, for instance, wanted a thousand-word essay. But it was Father Brody whose freshman assignment sparked rebellion.

Saying he was dissatisfied with their progress through Caesar's *Conquest of Gaul*—"You people haven't even mastered the declensions!"—he demanded they translate *3,000* lines over Christmas: "And I want them accurate, too. No more lollygagging, gentlemen!"

He delivered this as if startled by his own forcefulness. The boys looked at one another in disbelief.

Leaving with a cheery, "Enjoy your holidays!" Father Brody added, "And see you at the Bacchanal later. Yes, I'm this year's chaperone."

— *THE HOLY HUGS OF FATHER S.* —

At lunch his assignment was the talk of the freshmen — rather, its undertone, Father Dooley busy ferreting out violators: "*Jug*, Mr. Dumont! *Jug*, Mr. Halloran!" But in furious whispers: "It's too much!" "That's a hundred pages of 3-holed paper!"

Jeff didn't say anything, but it rankled. Translating 3,000 lines would spoil hours of every vacation day. It was too much — objectively, just *too much*.

Moreover, he thought Father Tanner, the Headmaster, might agree.

There was no after-lunch recess; boys milled in the corridor or on the terrace for a few minutes, but at least were permitted to talk.

Jeff sought out Gerald, who was uncharacteristically angry about Father Brody's assignment.

Vance, too.

"Guys, let's go see Father Tanner," he told them, "and tell him it's too much."

Wha—! See Father *Tanner?* You didn't just *go see* the Headmaster. Tucked away in his office off the foyer, he was anyway doubtless unconcerned with such minutiae as homework assignments.

"And Father Brody would *know!*" Gerald protested. "He'd have it in for us the rest of the year. Hell, until we graduate!"

Henry Keating happened to pass.

"Henry!" Jeff said for the first time in his life. "I'm thinking of going to Father Tanner about Father Brody's assignment, and —"

"I'm in," said Henry. "Let's do it."

While their classmates went downstairs, they two trooped up the corridor, passing the stiff pantheon — *Class of 1921, Class of 1935, Class of 1947, Class of 1959.* Henry at his side, Jeff was in heaven, but couldn't speak to him.

They turned into the Headmaster's anteroom.

"We'd like to see Father Tanner, please," Jeff told his secretary.

This startled her, but she communicated something on the phone and directed them to a bench. Bells rang to signal the start of class period.

Henry nudged Jeff, his smile saying, "Here goes nothin'." Jeff smiled back.

Soon Father Tanner invited the boys into his office.

Jeff knew him only from his admission interview. The Headmaster had asked why he wished to attend Garrett Prep and Jeff, eyes unfocussed as though consulting his soul, answered, "For the love of learning."

Now, bolstered by Henry's presence, he made their case, informing the Headmaster of Father Brody's assignment and comparing it to his much shorter Thanksgiving one, while acknowledging the greater length of Christmas vacation. It was simple, articulate and conveyed no grievance that the priest assigned homework, only protested that, as possibly Father Brody didn't realize, 3,000 lines was *too much*.

"Too much," echoed Henry.

Father Tanner stood up, shook their hands and said, "Better get to class. Mrs. Gifford will give you late cards."

The boys hurried downstairs.

"You did very well," Henry told Jeff.

"Well, we tried," Jeff replied, shrugging. What did failure, or even 3,000 lines, matter next to being friends with Henry?

They proffered their late cards as they went into

THE HOLY HUGS OF FATHER S.

Algebra.

In the final class period—by Jeff's reckoning, three Henry nods and four Henry smiles later—shortly before the Bacchanal was to commence, Father Brody stepped into the classroom.

"Mr. Lawrence, may I?" he said from the doorway to the novitiate auditing student speeches.

Shambling in, he looked angry, his face a patchy red.

"Well, guess you can't take it," he said. "*I don't care*—it's *your* knowledge of Latin at stake. OK: Cutting back the Christmas assignment. Start on page 67, line 5, and translate through page 72, line 15." He flipped pages back and forth. "Just 300 lines, all right? But remember, *accuracy.*"

He closed his book, nodded at the teacher and left, while the boys ululated with glee, hands reaching to pat Jeff's and Henry's backs.

SOON THEY WERE at the Bacchanal. All students attended, but by design Jesuits were absent save for a designated chaperone. The party was meant to let the boys blow off steam, to cram the manic excitements of Christmas and hormones into an explosive but private 90 minutes.

The gym, hung with balloons and bunting as for a dance, featured tables set out with soft drinks, apple cider and Christmas goodies. The P.A. throbbed with Beatles, Temptations and Four Tops.

The highlight every year was the varsity and junior varsity football teams' fabled can-can line of high-kicking boys in wigs, lipstick, balloon breasts, pleated skirts and no underwear; everybody knew to avoid the locker room that afternoon. When the players poured onto the floor, arms around one another's waists and kicking high to the Stones' *Let's Spend The Night Together,* they revolved like a Busby Berkeley chorus line amidst hoots and catcalls ("Powell, you're so pretty!" "Fitzgerald, you're a 10!"), and inspired the other boys to dance—not with one another, oh no!—but to frug in a frenzy by themselves.

Jeff frugged away, happy that engineering the homework rebellion cemented him into the school at last, made his semester a success. When the can-can line broke up, he found Henry frugging near by to *Ticket to Ride,* fetching in his plaid skirt, lipstick, a curly wig. Jeff had to smile, and Henry smiled back, and they frugged together to song after song.

When the lights finally went up the P.A. switched to *Silent Night,* and the whole corps of Jesuits entered to shake every boy's hand and wish him a Merry Christmas. Jeff saw Father Brody crossing the floor towards them—no, towards *Henry,* his expression less resentful than determined.

As Jeff left to catch the school bus, he looked back, but the priest's cassock blotted out the sight of his friend.

24.

As the days grew short, Father Schmidt tried not to think about the delights of Christmas season at St. Jude's.

St. Jude's always held elaborate Advent services—a delightful spiritual tease—and its choir sang special programs at the Shrine of the Immaculate Conception, where Father would pinch himself at being in the big time for sure. There was also the box truck rented for the choir to go caroling in Teagers Mill Estates, Storybook Forest and other developments, boys hopping off the rear to sing like angels in red felt hoods in front of parishioners' homes, before being stuffed with hot chocolate and cookies. Not to mention all the parish parties, cocktail and otherwise, nor the Bazaar, nor Midnight Mass, the church filled to overflowing to hear Johnny Capistrano sing *It Came Upon the Midnight Clear*.

But Father wasn't at St. Jude's any longer, but at St. Datian's, deep in Southern Maryland, alone, depressed and dependent on his friend Father Robin for access to boys.

Still, he liked eating out with Father Robin, losing

quarters in slot machines or raking in jackpots (proprietors tended to tip off the priests when one was due).

But home he would come to his own dank rectory. Diligent as his housekeeper was, it never really looked clean. On top of everything else, his parishioners proved resistant to Vatican II's innovations—were vociferous about preferring their Mass in Latin, about wanting Father to stand up there chanting incantations at the wall instead of speaking English to their faces.

And the TV reception! But it's amazing what you can get used to. Father Schmidt would sit for hours watching ghosts move back and forth.

His lowest point came the December afternoon he was gunning the Fury along the water's edge and ran over something that caused a blowout that had him embracing the steering wheel for dear life. And that was just the start of it. He got home at last furious and filthy.

Home.

But he knew what the season demanded, so from the pulpit invited everybody to a Christmas party in the parish hall on Friday evening, the day before Christmas Eve.

And as it happened, that Christmas party proved the turning point for Father Schmidt, pointed the way to how he would prosper in St. Mary's County for the next 30 years.

He festooned the hall behind the church with streamers, crêpe-paper reindeer and a crèche he found in the attic. Also he brought in a Christmas tree, strung lights on it and hung it with colored-glass globes and tinsel.

Parishioners attended in force, and were good enough to bring platters of cookies, bourbon balls, peanut brittle, fudge, fruitcakes.

—THE HOLY HUGS OF FATHER S.—

But it was Father's fruit punch that made the party go. He made it in a galvanized garbage can, with Father Robin's help cutting up painfully-procured strawberries, oranges, lemons, grapes, grapefruit, apples and cherries, adding orange juice, pineapple juice, cranberry juice, grapefruit juice and—bourbon. So much bourbon? *That* was the secret.

While carving up fruit Father Schmidt lamented how the boys of St. Martin's seemed so much friendlier than those of St. Datian's.

Scoffing, Father Robin gave him a pep talk.

"You've got loads of local talent," he informed his friend. "See it on every visit—drives me crazy, in fact.

"What is it I've been telling you? *Loosen up!* Loosen up and be a little brave, and you'll find everything you want right at your feet!"

The punch—enticingly blood-red in the crystal punchbowl, lemon slices floating persuasively on top—was a hit. And within minutes of ladling out the first cups—to adults only, of course—hubbub arose to hilarious new heights. The punch carried a punch.

When Father started a Christmas carol sing-along, everybody joined in, laughing hysterically when they forgot the words or missed the high notes.

As parishioners began to stagger off homeward, humming, the chagrinned parents of a sturdy lad of 14 named Lucas apologized for his "getting into" the punch (Father Robin had plied him with it until he couldn't speak or do anything but eat out lemon slices with a lopsided grin on his face), and readily agreed to Father Schmidt's suggestion (it was Father Robin's idea) that he stay the night to sleep it off.

He did so in Father Schmidt's bed.

In the morning, after pounding at the gates of heaven all night, Father Schmidt realized that St. Datian's just might do, after all.

He soon concluded an arrangement with Lucas's parents, hiring the boy to answer the rectory telephone after school. The parents were gratified that their son could thus pile up spiritual brownie points while making a little money; his mother hoped it would help him discern a vocation, for she longed to have a priest for a son. And Father made the most of Lucas's company.

Thus began Father Schmidt's 30-year, unbroken string of adolescent male phone-answerers. Whenever one left—Father assuring him his wife would be glad of what Father had taught him—he got to choose a new boy and break him in, show him how bodies work. It was a delicious cycle.

25.

CHRISTMAS EVE, the Osbornes' telephone rang. It was Carol's cousin Bunny calling from home, with Hortense on the extension.

"Carol, something you should know," said Bunny. "We discussed whether we should even tell you."

"Tell me what?"

"Krameria's for sale. Opened the *Post* this morning, and there it was in the real estate classifieds!"

"No!"

"10234 Krameria, brick Tudor, two bedrooms, garage? $25,000."

A world seemed to open up to Carol. Her mother had lived there for eleven years. It was a solid, pretty house, with French doors to a patio and a beautiful lawn dominated by a Douglas fir.

Carol felt a special bond because, inheriting part of her father's estate shortly after her mother bought it, she paid off the mortgage for her — happy to be able to do so. Her parents having divorced when she was a toddler, Carol never knew her father, who remarried and prospered.

Her mother paid $15,000 for the house, which, her sole heir, Carol more than recouped when she sold it.

That evening, handing Jeff a glass of eggnog, Carol said, "Honey, Bunny and Hortense called earlier to tell me Grandmother's house is on the market. Do you remember it?"

"Of course. Great house."

"Well, I'm thinking of buying it back and moving in."

"You always said you didn't want to live in Denver!"

"I think now I might feel more at home there. In fact, I know I will."

"Mother, what about *me?*"

"You can board at Prep if you want.

"I think it'll work out, Jeff. It's a good deal, too. *This* house I expect we can get $60,000 for, even more—maybe 70 or 75. Should clear enough that you can board at Prep until you graduate."

"Thank you, Mother."

Early Christmas morning Carol and Jeff trekked out to Dulles and enjoyed an empty flight to Denver. There, Bunny feeding them Christmas dinner, Carol laughed more than in a long time, mainly at jokes at her expense about the stay at the Outer Banks. *The Back of Beyond,* her cousins called it.

Next day, they toured the house on Krameria, confirming that it was in the same fine condition as when Carol sold it in 1961. The new owners had made improvements, too: The kitchen had a dishwasher and new cabinets. Carol made an all-cash offer subject to the usual contingencies, and it was accepted. Closing would take place in late January or early February, after inspections and a title search.

Hortense and Bunny insisted on taking Jeff to see Denver's own Jesuit high school, Regis.

Meanwhile he did some hard thinking over Christmas, even as, though finding no joy in Caesar, he completed his assignments.

He thought: *I begin to suspect that I'll do best — get where I'm going, wherever that is — if I reject everything they tell me or try to teach me. My instinct may be wobbly, but it's what I have.*

Jeff knew he had to figure out how to live his life — climb out of that deep well of shame his Church and his priest had plunged him into — and make it *his* life, one he wanted to live, and that he had to do it by himself. But instinct told him Henry could help.

So though he'd always think of himself as one of life's slow learners, Jeff did some of the work towards knowing himself that was crucial to accepting himself, too.

And serenely awaited his return to Prep. After a week's classes, there would be a week of exams, followed by another weeklong break. Then he could move into the dorm. About the only thing he liked about Prep was that Henry was there. But that was enough, for, miraculously, connection had been made. He was in love. Maybe they could room together?

Meanwhile he enjoyed Denver. It's a handsome city and, for a kid a few years shy of getting a drivers license, an easy one to get around. Buses head down Colfax Avenue every few minutes.

What Father Schmidt crushed? Jeff could feel it beginning to come back to life, spring back into shape.

He and his mother returned to Washington with lightened hearts.

CLASSES RESUMED ON a dark winter's day as snow fell on the morning rush hour. Jeff tingled with anticipation.

Homeroom that morning bustled with boys showing off new sport coats, ties, watches in the dreary basement bleached with fluorescent light. But Henry wasn't there. His desk was empty. Where Jeff was accustomed to have his shapely head in fuzzy focus was a space that stayed empty however often he looked. When Dr. Lister read the roll, he omitted Henry's name.

The door rattled. Jeff glanced over, sure it was Henry, but it was Woodrow coming in with a late card.

Dr. Lister's class gave way to Mr. Finian's. Afterwards, at the break before Latin, Jeff sought out Henry's roommate, Joe Durkin. That it might be hard lines on Joe for Jeff to try to snatch up his roommate for his own was something he hadn't thought of.

He asked where Henry was.

"Proctor says he's not coming back," Joe told him.

Jeff was thunderstruck. "Leaving before the end of the semester? *Why?*"

"I don't know," said Joe. "His stuff's gone."

Jeff asked for Henry's address, but Joe didn't know it.

"Where's he from, anyway?"

"California someplace. Los Angeles, maybe? San Francisco?"

Jeff stared, then—boys around them quaffing Teem and tearing into Snickers bars—vaulted upstairs to the Headmaster's office.

He greeted Mrs. Gifford—she looked up at him benignly—and asked for Henry Keating's home address.

"Oh, we can't give that out," she told him.

— *THE HOLY HUGS OF FATHER S.* —

He just made it back to the classroom before Latin, walking in with Mr. Finian.

Mr. *Finian?* But they'd just *had* English.

"All right, gentlemen, take your seats."

"Mr. Finian, this is *Latin,*" Woodrow said helpfully. "Father *Brody's* class."

"Don't tell me you jokers don't know I teach Latin, too?" Mr. Finian replied merrily, as though playing a secret joke. "Upper form? If I can do *that,* I *think* I can cope with *you* squirts. No, you'll have *me* to put up with twice a day from now on. *Ha!*

"Please hand up your Christmas assignments and open your textbooks — *Latin* textbooks — to page 74."

"Where's Father Brody?" several asked.

Mr. Finian looked knowing.

"Good question. No, actually I can tell you that Father Brody's not at Prep any longer. He's been reassigned to Woodstock."

Woodstock College was the Jesuit seminary near Baltimore.

For a moment Jeff wondered whether the rebellion he co-captained had so discouraged the priest that he fled Prep.

Then it hit him. Henry Keating and Father Brody both gone? He felt sick.

Worse, what if the rebellion had made his co-captain the priest's target?

"All right, gentlemen, still in Caesar, I'm afraid. Got it, Randy? Read from line 16?"

Mr. Finian took up a proprietary stance over the boy, an easy reach for him. Slipping his fingers into his shirt, he undid a button, then, thumbing down the yoke of his undershirt, enjoyed at last, after such extended holidays, the bliss of cupping a boy's breast, of stiffening his nipple.

Clenching his jaw and flushing red, Randy piped, "*Pharus est in insula turris magna altitudine, mirificis operibus exstructae; quae nomen ab insula accepit.*"

"Who can translate?" asked Mr. Finian. "Anyone? Anyone?"

26.

IN TIME FATHER SCHMIDT expanded St. Datian's, building a new rectory and founding a parish school. Also he began driving Chryslers, a new one every other year.

For beginning in about 1970 Southern Maryland underwent a wondrous transformation. New roads, bridges and schools attracted Washingtonians to visit or build second homes, even move there and commute to the capital. Washington, D.C.'s perpetual prosperity at last washed generously over the region.

In fact, the afternoon a knock came at the rectory door and he dispatched young Freddy to answer it, Father was admiring renderings of the new church he proposed building at last. They reminded him of seeing the first renderings of St. Jude's, back when the new parish was still holding Mass in the cafeteria of Good Shepherd High School. The completed buildings never looked so glamorous as the renderings, and Father—looking at the bell tower soaring beneath pastel skies of fluffy clouds, stylized pedestrians passing in the foreground—sighed to think such would be the fate of the new St. Datian's, too.

Freddy returned with two detectives and two policemen who arrested Father Schmidt on child sex abuse charges, handcuffed him and carried him off to jail.

Lucas, Father Schmidt's very first phone answerer, gray-haired now, but still crippled by the abuse he suffered, had come forward. Others bravely followed — in the end, more than *twenty* others. Father pleaded guilty to several charges, was sentenced to sixteen years in prison, and removed from the priesthood.

He even served four-and-a-half hellish months, before the judge reduced his sentence to time served and sent him to live at the Church's bucolic Vianney Renewal Center in Dittmer, Missouri, far from any boys.

There, Father Schmidt eventually died at the ripe old age of 83.

www.ingramcontent.com/pod-product-compliance
Lightning Source LLC
LaVergne TN
LVHW041844070526
838199LV00045BA/1429